ALSO BY CHRISTINE MCDONNELL

Don't Be Mad, Ivy
Toad Food & Measle Soup
Lucky Charms & Birthday Wishes

Count Me In

• A NOVEL BY •
Christine McDonnell

VIKING KESTREL

VIKING KESTREL
Viking Penguin Inc., 40 West 23rd Street, New York, New York 10010, U.S.A.
Penguin Books Ltd, Harmondsworth, Middlesex, England
Penguin Books Australia Ltd, Ringwood, Victoria, Australia
Penguin Books Canada Limited, 2801 John Street, Markham, Ontario, Canada L3R 1B4
Penguin Books (N.Z.) Ltd, 182–190 Wairau Road, Auckland 10, New Zealand

Copyright © Christine McDonnell, 1986
All rights reserved
First published in 1986 by Viking Penguin Inc.
Published simultaneously in Canada
Printed in USA
by The Book Press, Brattleboro, Vermont
Set in Sabon
1   2   3   4   5   90   89   88   87   86

Library of Congress Cataloging in Publication Data
McDonnell, Christine.   Count me in.
Summary: Thirteen-year-old Katie has a difficult time adjusting to her
new family situation, especially after her mother and new stepfather announce
that they are expecting a baby.
[1. Remarriage—Fiction]   I. Title.
PZ7.M47843Co   1986   [Fic]   85-40834   ISBN 0-670-80417-7

For Anne Dunham

Families

From her corner seat, Katie watched Ruth writing a long note on a piece of paper that she'd torn from her spiral notebook. She folded it into a tiny wedge, wrote a name on the front, and palmed it to the girl on her right. Looking up, she gestured to Katie that it was for her. It passed from hand to hand, up the side row. Just as the boy in the last seat tossed it across to the next desk, Miss Miller turned around from the board and spotted it immediately.

"Bring the note up here, please." Miss Miller's voice was calm but cold.

Bud Roche stumbled up the aisle and handed over the tiny square.

"I didn't write it," he said.

"Thank you, Bud." She dismissed him with a nod.

The class waited. Would she read it out loud?

Katie leaned her face on her hands, feeling the hot blush against her palms. Oh, Ruth, you dummy.

Miss Miller smiled thinly and began to unfold it.

If she had a mustache, she'd twirl the end, Katie thought. Ruth, what did you say?

Miss Miller cleared her throat dramatically. "'Hey Katie. How's it going, pal? This class is boring. Can't wait for lunch. School stinks.'"

At this, Miss Miller raised her eyebrows, feigning surprise. Then she continued.

"'So what's the story? Do you like Jimmy Moran? You say he's just a friend, but I think you really like him. Come on, admit it. Tell your pal Ruthy, better known as Lorna Love-love, the gossip queen.'"

Miss Miller paused again. Several people giggled. Katie kept her eyes on her desk. I'll kill you, Ruth, she thought.

But the note still wasn't finished. "'Hey, Miss Miller's slip is showing. Aren't her shoes witchy? Why does she always wear that rose perfume? I hate it. Come over after school, okay? Love ya, Ruthie.'"

Miss Miller had a half smile that could be either amusement or annoyance. She folded the note and tucked it in her pocket. "Thank you for sharing that with us, Ruth."

The class chuckled nervously, a little embarrassed.

"And now, class, back to the topic. The last unit we'll do this year is on families, the basic component of society."

Miss Miller smiled. Katie nodded back, almost as a reflex. Even though Miss Miller was strict, she liked her directness and her sense of humor. She always talked

2:

rapid-fire, shooting out words and ideas so fast that Katie seldom got bored. She never made them memorize dates the way they had in seventh grade.

Miss Miller pointed to a collection of photographs of different families, large and small. Under each picture, in different handwriting, were the words "We are a family."

"What makes a group of people a family? Do they have to be related? Can one person alone be a family?" Miss Miller asked her usual string of questions.

Katie listened but kept her hand down. She wasn't willing to get involved. Does it matter? she thought. A family's something you're stuck with. You can't do anything about it.

Katie's mind drifted as Miss Miller talked. On her notebook she drew a stick-figure family: a mother with curly cartoon hair, a father with a beard, two kids, a dog, and a cat. She started listening again when it sounded like homework. The first assignment was to write a family profile.

"Immediate family plus grandparents, aunts, uncles, first cousins, stepparents, and stepbrothers and stepsisters, too. I know some of you have parents who have divorced and remarried, so you'll have a bigger immediate family to describe."

Katie looked down at her desk, not wanting to meet Miss Miller's gaze. Some of us wish we didn't, she thought.

Ruth waited for her in the hall at the end of class. They'd walked home together after school every afternoon since first grade.

"Sorry about the note," Ruth said. "I thought she'd keep writing on the board."

Katie shrugged. She wasn't upset anymore. "Jimmy

Moran is just a friend. That's the last time I'm going to tell you."

"Okay, okay. Just checking. Got to keep up with romances. Want to eat over? It's lasagna. Mom said to ask you, since you like it so much. We could get started on the family project."

When she got home, Katie called her mother at work to tell her she was eating at Ruth's. The house was empty and peaceful. She felt comfortable being alone there, especially in the afternoon when the late winter sun warmed the rooms. She changed into jeans and a sweatshirt, fed the goldfish, watered her geranium, stuffed a legal pad into her backpack, and rode her bike the three blocks to the Iveses' house.

She found Ruth upstairs, sitting on her bed. Her room was strewn with books and clothes. Katie picked a path through the mess and sat down in Ruth's rocking chair, displacing a pair of jeans, an army shirt, and two scarves. Ruth was thumbing through a stack of photo albums.

"Want to see my parents when they first got married? They look goofy."

The photo showed a couple standing on a mountaintop with wind blowing their hair back off their faces. Squinting against the sun, they grinned into the camera. Katie looked at the picture closely, trying to connect these two kids with the people who sat at the ends of the Iveses' dinner table and talked so intensely about politics and books.

"Your mother looks just like you."

"It's weird, isn't it?" Ruth picked up her hair and piled it on top of her head. She made a long, serious face and said

4:

in a low voice, "I wish you'd find something else to wea. besides those jeans."

"She's wearing jeans, herself, here," Katie pointed out. "Are you going to use these with your report?"

"Maybe one with the whole family at the reunion last year."

She turned the pages, passing photos of smiling babies, toddlers naked at the beach, kids in Halloween costumes, and a variety of Christmas trees. She stopped at a large group picture.

The family was posed in front of a rambling white house with a round turret. The front porch steps were wide, seating eight people on each riser. Children and dogs sat on the grass in front while the grown-ups clustered around a tiny, regal, white-haired lady. She held a big-eyed baby with a bald head.

"That's Granny holding my cousin Alicia. The oldest and the youngest."

The picture triggered a twinge of envy in Katie. The Ives family was a fortress, fortified by numbers. Katie often thought how great it must be to be one of eight. Ruth had older sisters to answer important questions, and older brothers to threaten her enemies.

"Where are your sisters?" she asked.

Ruth pointed them out in the crowd: Grace, Ellen, and Pamela.

"Remember when Pamela told us the facts of life?" Katie said.

"And you didn't believe her?" teased Ruth.

She'd told them one day as they lay on their stomachs on the hot cement by the town pool. Katie and Ruth were going into fourth grade. Pamela was eleven.

"That part of your father fits into your mother just like an extension cord."

Pamela's words floated hazily above Katie's head like the air shimmering above the ground during a heat wave. Gradually Katie understood what Pamela meant. The thought bolted her into a sitting position.

"You're nuts! That isn't the way it happens," she said.

"Oh, yes, it is. It most certainly is," Pamela retorted with smug conviction. "Just ask your mother if you don't believe me."

Later, she and Ruth discussed it, treading water in the swimming pool.

"Do you believe it?" Katie asked.

"Sure. Why not? The sperm's got to get to the egg somehow, doesn't it?" Ruth said, unruffled.

But Katie felt shocked by the sudden invasion of news. She hadn't thought much about sex before. Once, when she was in kindergarten, she and Richard, the boy next door, had pulled down their pants in the garage.

Katie smiled at the memory. It seemed a very long time ago.

Ruth kept on flipping through the photos, but Katie, losing interest, reached for a magazine.

"How's this for a father?" She showed Ruth an ad for perfume, featuring a distinguished dark-haired man with an eye patch and a mustache. "He'll be a diplomat who travels all over the world."

"What's your mother going to be like?"

"Wait a minute. I'll find her." Katie kept leafing the pages. "She'll be beautiful but homey. The kind who makes brownies. But she's still sophisticated, not just some housewife. Maybe she's a designer."

"Hey," Ruth said. "Let's make up pretend families using magazine pictures. That'll be more fun than writing our own."

"We need more magazines," said Katie.

"There's some in the den." Ruth closed the album.

By the time Mrs. Ives called them to set the table, they had each assembled four different families, complete with children, houses, some furniture, occupations, and definite personalities.

Ruth's favorite family had a mother with pink hair, a father on a motorcycle, a grandmother in a flowered bathing suit and a straw hat, and two babies with no clothes on at all. Katie's had a tweedy father with horn-rimmed glasses, a mother in a diamond tiara, two teenage boys playing football, and a sheepdog.

"The mother adds a note of glamour, but it's really an ordinary family," she explained.

"Who wants ordinary?" said Ruth. "I want weird."

As soon as Mr. Ives got home and changed out of his suit, Mrs. Ives called, "Dinner, everyone," and the children filtered down from their rooms and took their places.

Katie glanced around the table. When the Iveses held hands for the silent blessing, they were like a stand of tall trees, rooted together. Divorce would never splinter them the way it had her tiny family.

"Pass the bread, please, Katie," asked Ruth's oldest brother, Tom.

All the brothers were tall, dark-haired, and quiet, except for Skip, the youngest, who was always teasing for attention, tagging after Ruth and Katie, trying to listen in on their private conversations. Once, Skip had even climbed out on the roof above Ruth's window, trying to hear what the girls were saying to each other.

Last year, in seventh grade, Katie had had a crush on Dave, who was fifteen and six feet tall. This year, Dave had a girlfriend named Suzannah, and Katie's crush had faded gradually. Now she hardly remembered the rushing awkwardness she'd felt. She could be in the same room with him and not even blush or stammer. Tonight she sat across from him and managed to smile easily, returning his jokes.

After dinner, Katie and Ruth rinsed the dishes and loaded the dishwasher. It was Skip's night on the pots and pans.

"I better go," Katie said when they'd finished. "I've got to get started on the project for real."

"We should hand in these phony families. Maybe she'll give us extra credit," Ruth said. "They're much more interesting." She picked up the pink-haired mother. "This mother would let me get another hole in each ear. She'd probably let me get my hair cut punk, too."

"I bet she'd even let you get your nose pierced," Katie said. "You could wear a safety pin through it."

"Gross." Ruth rubbed her nose protectively. "Are you going to use pictures in your real family profile?"

"Maybe. I have to ask my mother where they are. I think they're all packed away in the attic." Katie pulled on her sweatshirt and packed her cut-out families carefully between the pages of the legal pad.

"Why?"

"I guess she didn't want them around. They show my dad a lot. Maybe she thought they'd hurt Steve's feelings."

8:

Ruth nodded. "That makes sense."

"Not to me. Just because she wants to forget all that doesn't mean I do. I'm going to ask her for them."

Katie could tell from Ruth's startled face that her voice had been angry. It was leaking out again, all that anger. She just couldn't seem to keep it in.

The Profile

Since it wasn't due for a while, Katie didn't look at the project sheet again until the next day after dinner. She was sitting at her desk. Downstairs, she could hear Steve running water, rattling pans and closing cupboard doors as he put things away. It was his turn to clean up.

"First, write a description of the people in your immediate family, the people you live with. Try to capture their personalities. Include both your parents, even if you do not live with them both. For your extended family include only those people you have actually met. Give a one- or two-line description of each. Limit this part to ten people.

"Then answer this question: What do you like most about being a member of your family?"

Katie took out a fresh sheet of paper and wrote at the

top, "Family Profile: Katie Henderson." She decided to start with her mother.

"Mother: Madeline Norton (used to be Madeline Henderson). Nickname: Maddie. Brown hair, blue eyes, wears glasses when she reads."

She chewed on the end of her pen.

"She likes to read and to cook. She has a good sense of humor, but she gets mad sometimes. Once she threw a whole bowl of salad at my father. She used to like movies and bike riding. Now she's married and she does things with her husband, like go to concerts."

What a dumb assignment. She stared at the paper a little longer and then put her mother aside for later. She took out a fresh sheet.

"Father: Ed Henderson. Photographer. Works for a news service. Travels a lot. Lives in the city. Tall, red hair, beard. Loves to laugh and eat Chinese food (but not at the same time)."

Katie smiled as she thought of Ed. He was a long-legged, gangly sort of person. He loved rock and roll, and he quoted songs all the time. "Sugar pie, honey bun," he would sing to her as if it were her name. He always wore jackets with lots of pockets, and he filled them with film and lenses so they bulged. He rode a ten-speed bike around the city and called hello to people that he passed, even if he didn't know them.

But how could she say all that? There was too much to put in. Better start with Steve. Since she didn't know him so well, maybe he'd be easier.

"Stepfather: Stephen Norton. Skinny. Brown hair. Blue eyes. Occupation: Physicist. Likes classical music."

She chewed on her pen again. There was a lot she could

say, but was it important? Likes the bathroom sink spotless. Watches the news on TV every night. Wears pants with perfect creases.

Everything about Steve was crisp and exact, even the way he organized his desk with sharpened pencils in a row, yellow pads on the right. When he set the table, the napkins were perfect triangles.

What did Miss Miller care about the way somebody set the table?

She put down her pen and closed her notebook. I'll ask Ruth what she's putting in, Katie decided. She started on her math homework instead.

Big News

After a long, cold March, the warm April days were welcome. Katie stayed outside as much as possible, enjoying the sweet air and sense of freedom. She loved the change of seasons. Now, early spring made her whistle and even break into a skip when no one was looking.

It was almost six when she got home from riding bikes with Ruth. They'd cycled all afternoon, going nowhere special—out to the reservoir, around the park with the three hills, and in and out through all the streets in their neighborhood. When the sun began to set and the air grew chilly, they headed home.

Katie put her bike in the garage, careful to lean it against the wall, away from Steve's car. She tried to smooth her hair, hopelessly bushy and tangled from the wind. She had to set the table, and she was late. Draping her jacket on the doorknob of the front hall closet, she hurried into the dining room, the glow of sun and wind still on her face.

Tonight she planned to ask Maddie about the camping trip. She'd been working up her nerve. It was a trip they'd planned long before Maddie had ever met Steve. "Remember that trip out West you always promised me? You said we'd go cross-country, camping out in the parks. That's what I'd like for my graduation present." She rehearsed the lines in her mind. They'd talked about the trip for years. Why not this summer?

To her surprise, the table was already set with china and even champagne glasses, flowers in the cut-glass vase, new candles. Set for three, the table looked awkward to her. Two was more symmetrical, more balanced.

"Wash your hands, honey. Dinner's just about ready," Maddie called from the kitchen.

Steve and Maddie were already seated when Katie came back in. Maddie grinned secretively at Steve. He returned the smile. They tossed their smiles back and forth over Katie's head, a game of catch for two.

"What's up?" she said.

Maddie finally broke the suspense. "We're going to have a baby."

Steve uncorked the champagne bottle with a loud pop.

"A baby? When did you find out? When's it due?" Katie said, and then added, "Congratulations!" She smiled and nodded as she listened to the details, sipping the champagne carefully. If she had too much, she might show her confusion. But they were so excited, she doubted they would notice anything. Inside, she felt numb. She still hadn't gotten used to Steve's being in the house, and now, a baby!

After dinner, she lay on her bed with her face buried in her cool pillow. Thoughts whirled around in her mind, fragments of conversations, images of babies she'd known. After a few minutes, she rolled over on her back and folded her arms behind her head. This sure canceled the camping trip. There wasn't any point in even asking about it. The baby wasn't exactly a surprise. She'd guessed it would come sooner or later. Someone even mentioned it at the wedding.

The wedding! Every time she thought about it, she cringed. First she'd had to walk down the aisle, shaking knees making her teeter on the high heels. She was positive dark half-circles of perspiration stained the silly ruffled bridesmaid dress and everyone noticed. At the reception she drank three glasses of champagne and stopped caring what everybody thought. The bubbles went up her nose, and she sneezed on the first glass.

"Take it easy on the bubbly," her mother had whispered. But Katie downed two glasses before the toast. She tried not to look as the groom kissed the bride. But she knew she was blushing.

It seemed as if everyone she'd talked to all evening had to tell her how wonderful Steve was. They were trying to convince her, hinting that she should be nice to him.

The champagne had made her dizzy, and she'd gone to the ladies' room to wash her face. She was sitting in a stall, resting her head on her knees when she heard two women come in.

"It won't be easy living with a thirteen-year-old," one said.

"Don't be so negative. He loves kids. You know, if anyone can get along with a teenager, it's Steve. Anyway, I bet we hear news of a baby before the year's out."

That was the first time anyone had mentioned a baby. Now it was on the way. What had her mother said tonight? We're going to have a baby. We. All of us? Or just you and him? It's not *we*, it's *you*, Katie thought. *You're* going to have a baby. It doesn't have a thing to do with me.

She thumped the bed with her fist, knocking her old teddy bear onto the floor. He looked back at her with patient glass eyes. She lifted him off the floor and gave him a hug.

She knew she wasn't being fair or reasonable. Who cares? she thought. Was it fair for them to go away on vacation, leaving her with a baby-sitter who made her eat hot cereal every morning for the whole week? They sent her a postcard of the beach in Aruba while she was freezing her fanny off, walking to school every day. Was that fair?

"We need time alone, honey. People who haven't been married long need privacy," Maddie tried to explain.

"I think it's romantic," Ruth said when she heard. "They probably want more time for sex, I bet."

Katie didn't even want to think about that. The whole thing made her uncomfortable.

Ruth had been right. This proved it. Now everyone would know. As soon as the pregnancy started to show more, everyone in the whole wide world would know.

She thought about the cut-out families she'd assembled

at Ruth's, still safely packed in the pages of the yellow pad. She dug them out and lined them up on the desk top. Four mothers. One wore the diamond tiara. One wore jeans. One looked like an aging punk-rock star, with black hair in a crown of spikes. Ruth had made her cut her out so her pink-haired mother could have a friend. The last was in jogging clothes. Not one was pregnant.

For the next few days, Katie tried the silent treatment. It put off having to talk to Maddie. Be cool, she told herself, aloof, above it all. Speak only when spoken to.

Yes.

Uh-huh.

Okay.

Nothing's wrong.

No, thanks.

The silent treatment kept Maddie and Steve away, but it couldn't protect Katie from the world around her— crocuses opening, new buds filling out the trees, birds returning, sun warming the steps and sidewalk: spring. It all reminded her of her mother and the new baby coming.

Steve had been singing a song all week, about the baby making three.

And that leaves me out, Katie thought.

Sleeping Over

Ever since third grade, Katie and Ruth had alternated Friday-night sleepovers at each other's houses. At Ruth's, the bustle of brothers and sisters, the marathon Monopoly games, arguments, jokes, and teasing filled the evening. They usually stayed up too late and spent Saturday in a fog. At Katie's, there was privacy and plenty of time to talk. They often pretended they were visiting a hotel or having their hair done at the beauty parlor.

This Friday, Katie gladly headed over to Ruth's. Avoiding her mother's quizzical, slightly pleading gaze was difficult. Sometimes it felt as if Maddie could read her mind and knew all the small, jealous, angry thoughts that crowded in there these days.

Katie even felt bad about Steve. He just looked confused, as if he hadn't a clue why Katie was so sullen. He kept to himself, waiting for the mood to lighten.

Katie found Ruth experimenting with makeup. She sat in front of her mirror with her reading lamp beaming like a searchlight on her face.

Katie flopped on the bed. "I don't know how I can keep it up. She's going to be pregnant a long time."

Ruth drew a black line along the edge of her eyelid. "Yup. Nine months. What difference does it make if they're having a baby? Hand me that green eye shadow, will you?"

Katie sat up and passed her the round plastic container.

"What difference does it make? Don't you have any imagination? Dirty diapers, the kid crying all night, everybody going goo-goo, gaa-gaa. There'll be smelly, gooky ointment everywhere and powder all over the place. I know what it's going to be like. You might as well call me the live-in baby-sitter."

Ruth raised her eyebrows as she spread more color over her eyelids. "Okay, okay. Don't yell at me. I'm not the one having the baby." She rolled her eyes. "Luckily. My mother would have a fit."

Mrs. Ives was strict. Even this makeup was allowed only for play. "Wash it off, girls," Mrs. Ives always reminded them, even when it looked terrific. Even if they were just going to the movies, where they'd sit in the dark and no one could see it, the makeup had to come off.

"Which eye shadow do you like better, the green or the purple?" Ruth asked.

"You look like a vampire. Come on, let's go out."

"Why?"

"It's nice out. I want to ride bikes."

Ruth agreed to go, giving the mirror one last glance.

They headed out toward the lake, Katie in front. She pumped hard. The wind rushed against her face, and gradually the tightness inside relaxed.

"Race you to the bridge, start at the corner," she called back to Ruth.

Ruth pulled up even with her. They poised, waiting for the light to change. As the green lit up, they both started fast, bending low over the handlebars. Ruth's long legs whipped the pedals around, and she edged out in front.

"Loser pays for Cokes," she called.

Katie kept pumping, but Ruth's height gave her an advantage. She reached the bridge with a bike length to spare. To catch their breath, they circled the lake slowly, watching the changing patterns the wind made on the water.

"Do you think April is the cruelest month?" Ruth asked. "That's what some poet said."

"I wonder why he said that," Katie said.

"Beats me. You owe me a Coke. Let's go to Jack's."

They got a booth in the back, where Katie could watch the crowd. Sometimes Jack's made her feel like a little kid at a grown-ups' party. High-school kids looked so sure of themselves, the girls with their hair fixed just right, and the boys almost as big as men. Next to them, Katie felt small and self-conscious.

It was easier to come here with Ruth, though. Ruth with her long hair like a curtain and her quiet eyes. The high-school kids didn't worry her. Maybe that was because she had older brothers and sisters. She'd lift an eyebrow or make a funny face, and then she and Katie would both start to laugh.

The waitress came over. Ruth ordered a cherry Coke. Katie asked for hot chocolate.

"I still don't get why you're so upset," Ruth said when the waitress had left.

Katie struggled for the right words. It was hard to admit, even to Ruth, that she felt left out. It wasn't just the baby she was angry about. It was Steve coming in and turning things around.

After her father left, it was just Maddie and Katie. They'd been fine. They even went camping by themselves. They'd gone to the movies together. It was easy to find shows they both wanted to see—comedies, or romances with happy endings, or old mysteries.

At home, they'd sit in the living room reading, the room comfortably still, with only the sound of pages turning. Or they'd play double solitaire and eat popcorn, getting the cards greasy with the butter; nobody cared. Sometimes they danced. Maddie had taught her the lindy, the fox-trot, and the waltz.

Katie had always felt at ease in her house before Steve came. She took it for granted. She'd never even thought about it. She could go into any room, be part of any conversation. After all, it was her home.

Now she walked through the house like a guest unsure of a welcome. She hesitated on the stairs and in hallways, and coughed before going into rooms when Maddie and Steve were there, in case they were kissing or talking privately.

But how could she tell all this to Ruth, who never felt awkward or out of place? So she just shrugged. "I don't like babies, that's all."

Ruth looked at her suspiciously but didn't push it further. They finished their drinks, playing songs on the jukebox.

They got to the Iveses' just in time for dinner. Katie sat between Tom and Ruth, across from Dave. She ate here so often that she had her own place at the table. The family called the spare bed in Ruth's room Katie's bed.

"I met Maddie at Big Buy. She told me about the baby. You must be thrilled." Mrs. Ives beamed. "You're so lucky to have a baby coming. I really miss not having babies around anymore." She looked fondly at Skip, who was tall for ten and anything but a baby.

"Aw, cut it out, Mom," he complained.

Mr. Ives gazed at the ceiling with a look of practiced suffering. He'd heard this baby gush before. "Eight is plenty, dear. Sometimes eight is too much."

"I know, but still"— Mrs. Ives's voice grew wistful again—"I just love the way a baby feels. And that sweet baby smell."

Skip cut her off. "They smell like poop." Even though he usually complained about being the youngest, he thought having a baby in the family would be worse. "Do you want a baby, Katie? I wouldn't."

Katie squirmed on her chair, hating to be put on the spot. She took a swallow of water and tried to sound nonchalant. "It's just a baby. I'm not the one who's having it."

That night, Katie had trouble falling asleep. Even with the window open, Ruth's room was hot. At home, Maddie turned the heat down low at night.

22:

She kicked off her covers and lay staring at the dark window. She wished she could wake Ruth up and tell her everything.

Everything I do is wrong. I threw out the toothpaste cap by mistake, and Steve threw a fit. He complained about aqua dribbles for a week until Maddie chucked the tube and bought a new one. Even Maddie admits he's too fussy.

He called me an oaf when I spilled nail polish on his business magazine. He gets nervous when I even walk near his computer. And if I touch his records, he goes crazy. They're all arranged in this fancy filing system I can't understand. You wouldn't believe it.

Katie lay in the darkness a little longer, listening to Ruth snore lightly. When Ruth rolled over, the snoring stopped.

Katie turned her pillow over, rearranged the sheet, and tried to get comfortable. Telling Ruth won't do any good, she decided. I'd sound like a whiner. I've got to work it out myself, somehow.

A Summer Job

Katie put off the family profile until the last minute. On Thursday afternoon, unable to postpone it any longer, she took out the albums. She passed over pictures of her parents together and, instead, picked one of her mother standing alone on a rock in the middle of a cove, and one of her father wearing a baseball hat.

She flipped curiously through the pictures of her parents' wedding. People were making toasts, dancing, and laughing. Everybody was laughing, it seemed.

She studied the next pages more carefully, examining pictures of the three of them together when she was a baby, and then when she was first learning to walk, with one parent on each side of her, holding her hand and smiling. She searched their faces for signs of dissatisfaction.

24:

Looking through the years of pictures, Katie was struck by how much she looked like her father. Just the way Ruth looks like her mother, she thought. If she covered his beard and framed his face with her hands, it was her own face she saw.

Maybe I'm like him inside, too. I'm messy. I play my records loud, just like he does. Maybe that's why I don't fit in here.

The idea stayed in her mind as she worked on the profile. She finished it up after dinner, adding a little to her first draft and copying it quickly. She knew it was skimpy, but she didn't want to think about it anymore.

The next morning, she handed it in with a shake of her head.

"At least it's done," she said.

Miss Miller looked up with her eyebrows raised. "That's not very enthusiastic," she said with a quizzical smile.

Katie shrugged. "It was hard."

"It was meant to be fun."

"Maybe some people's families are fun. Mine isn't."

"I hadn't thought of that, Katie. I'll keep it in mind as I'm reading these. Maybe it was a harder assignment than I realized."

After school, Katie walked home with Ruth as usual.

"How was your discussion group?" Ruth asked. "Only four of us had nuclear families. How many in the step-family group?"

"Six.

"The single-parent group had eight. Only one person had an extended family," Katie said.

"No kidding. That's what my family will be next fall when my grandmother moves in. That's why Mom wants to talk to you and me. She's going to offer us a job painting Granny's rooms."

"She'll really pay us?"

"Yup, but Granny gets to pick the colors."

The rooms were in the back wing of the Iveses' house. One served as the kids' TV room, and the other was part playroom, part storage. The old rugs and faded wallpaper gave the rooms a dingy look that Katie had never noticed before. It had always been a comfortable place to play. You could make houses out of the furniture, use paint and glitter, and never worry about the mess.

Mrs. Ives described the job. "I've decided to strip the woodwork of all this old paint. I want you two to do the stripping and the painting. I'll do the plaster and the ceiling. We'll see how long it takes and than decide on a price. Okay?"

"I'm visiting my dad and my grandmother in August," Katie said.

"Then let's plan on working mornings in July before it gets too hot in the day. Start as soon after graduation as you like. Is it a deal?"

Both girls nodded.

Katie walked home slowly, enjoying the scent of lilacs. A real job. Wait until I tell Mom and Steve. I'll be so busy they won't even know I'm around.

Katie described the job at dinner.

"Scraping paint is hard," Maddie warned, and then added quickly, "but I'm sure you two can do it. You can keep each other company."

"I did a lot of that sort of thing in college," Steve said. "A group of us worked as house painters. Some tricks make scraping a lot easier. I'll come and show you if you're interested."

"Sure," said Katie, a little less enthusiastically than she'd meant. It was a habit she'd gotten into, sounding nonchalant rather than letting her real reaction show. Catching herself, she added, "That would be great."

Steve smiled. "It's small stuff—how long to leave the paint remover on and what type of steel wool to buy. We'll go to the hardware store before you start."

Katie nodded, surprised by his interest. "You really worked as a painter?"

"Sure. Every summer at the beach. We'd paint from seven until three or so, and then head for the water."

Over the next few days, Katie watched Steve more closely. The thought of his working as a painter didn't fit with the image she'd had of him, so neat and precise. So she watched. He seemed more relaxed. He even whistled some of her favorite songs.

"Why is Steve so happy lately?" she asked Maddie.

"I hadn't noticed anything different. Why not ask him yourself?"

So Katie did. Steve was sitting at the kitchen table after supper one night, looking through a gardening book and drawing diagrams of vegetable gardens, squares and rectangles divided into smaller areas.

Unable to think of a subtle way to put it, she blurted out, "You seem a lot happier lately." It was the most personal thing she'd ever said to him, and the minute it was out, she wished she could unsay it.

He looked up and grinned. "How can you tell?"

"You whistle. And you smile more." She hesitated, not

wanting to anger him. "And you don't get upset about things."

"Like what?"

"Music. The telephone. Things I do, like leaving my hair in the tub." She eyed him tentatively, waiting for his reaction.

"You heard me grumbling all the time?"

She nodded again.

He chuckled at himself. "The women in this family are too sharp. Did I sound like an ass? Barging in and complaining about everything? Did I?"

She shrugged. "What are you working on?" she asked instead.

"A plan for a vegetable garden in the back yard. What do you think of it?"

"I don't know anything about gardening."

"Me neither. This is strictly experimental. I'm planting everything I like. Snow peas, tomatoes, eggplant, peppers. What do you like?"

"Cucumbers, watermelon, corn, peas, I guess."

"We could plant those, too. Want to work on it with me?"

This time Katie hesitated only a second. "Sure," she said. It sounded like fun. She never had enough to do in the summer.

Steve beamed. "The ground's getting turned over this weekend. We'll dig in some manure and lime to give it a boost. Then it's planting time!"

Katie hadn't noticed how bouncy he got when he was excited.

He opened the book again. "Back to the drawing board. I'm glad you're in on this."

28:

Planting Seeds

Saturday morning, Katie woke to the roar of the Roto-tiller. She pulled on shorts she'd worn the day before and a clean T-shirt, splashed cold water on her face, brushed her teeth, combed her hair quickly with her fingers, and ran downstairs.

Steve had marked off the garden plot with stakes. Inside the square, a man was pushing the Rototiller along one edge.

Steve watched from the side of the plot. He had on cut-off jeans, old sneakers, and a baseball hat—the sloppiest clothes Katie had ever seen him wear. He waved and yelled over the motor, "What do you think? It's good soil."

Maddie came out carrying a tray with coffee, muffins,

and a bowl of cherries. "Breakfast!" she announced. She spread a blanket in the sun and poured mugs of coffee.

Katie took hers with lots of milk. She sipped it slowly as she watched the Rototiller churn up the last rows.

"Good spot for a garden," the man said when he finished. He wiped the sweat off his forehead with a wrinkled red bandanna. "Gonna be a scorcher."

Maddie offered him coffee, but he only took a muffin. Steve walked out to the truck with him and helped push the heavy machine up into the back. Katie and Maddie sat quietly enjoying the sun. Steve came back and sat cross-legged on the blanket.

"Okay, now we have to break up the big chunks with the rake or hoe and take out any rocks. Then we sprinkle the lime and fertilizer in and rake it. Then we can plant."

Breaking up clods was harder than Katie had expected. She chopped with the hoe, then smoothed the earth back, stopping to lob rocks onto the grass. Steve joined her, working with the heavy rake. As they moved down the rows, Maddie followed, throwing white lime in wide arcs on top of the soil.

"You look like a pioneer woman sowing grain," Steve said.

"That's me—Old Ma, working in the fields."

Steve unpacked the box from Wilson's Seeds: brown envelopes of seeds, wooden stakes to mark each row, a black waterproof pen to write on the stakes, and two odd tools.

"This gizmo's for lining up straight rows," Steve explained. "You stick one end in the ground, unravel the string as far as the row's going, then stick the other end in the dirt so the string is tight. It marks a straight line."

Maddie nodded, with a hint of laughter in her eyes. She thinks his neatness is a little nutty, too, Katie thought.

"This other one measures how deep each hole should be."

"You measure each hole?" Maddie asked.

Steve grinned. "I guess that's a little extreme. Maybe we can measure it row by row."

Katie watched and listened to the planting instructions as they moved along. Soon Steve's neat plan, labeled on graph paper, lay abandoned on the grass. Instead, they planted rows on whim, beans next to carrots, then peas.

They finished up after noon.

"Tired, dirty, but happy," said Steve. "Who's first in the shower?"

"You. You're the fastest," Maddie said.

Katie put the tools away while Maddie packed up the seed envelopes.

"Won't it be great to watch these grow?" Katie said as they walked toward the kitchen door. "I can't believe it all comes from those little seeds. It's like magic."

"The older I get, the more I believe in magic and miracles. Everything growing." Maddie gave Katie a one-armed hug.

Katie bumped against her before regaining her balance. The baby, she remembered suddenly, embarrassed by her awkwardness. She hadn't thought about it all morning.

Graduation Dress

The plants in the garden broke through the soil as fragile shoots. Slowly, miniature leaves unfurled, and the shoots grew into little plants.

Katie checked the calendar. Hanging on the refrigerator door, the calendar served as Maddie's appointment book and all-family organizer: Wed. June 3, Katie—dentist; Fri. June 5, Hank and Mary to dinner, *Rear Window* on Channel 5; Tues. June 9, obstetrician. June 16 was circled in red: Katie's graduation.

"I thought we'd look for your graduation dress today, and one for the dance, too. There isn't much time left," Maddie said. "We haven't gone shopping together in a while, have we?"

Katie shook her head, her mouth full of peanut butter.

They used to go every few months to get clothes for school or just to look around. They'd been almost the same size before, and tried on some of the same clothes, trading them back and forth in the dressing room. But that wouldn't happen now. She eyed Maddie's stomach surreptitiously, checking to see if the pregnancy showed yet.

Every bit of the pregnancy business bothered Katie: the support hose; the special vitamins in the center of the kitchen table; the books Maddie left around the house to try to get her interested.

She glanced through one when no one else was home. The photographs showed babies developing inside the womb, miniature beings with tiny fingers and transparent skin, curled up in the oval of the uterus, floating in an inner sea like magical sea creatures, water babies. In some pictures the baby looked like a very ancient man, wiser than anyone. In one, the baby was sucking its thumb with its eyes closed; it looked so vulnerable that Katie felt an urge to protect it from any harm. One picture corresponded exactly with the age of the baby inside Maddie. Katie studied it closely, fascinated by its completeness, and confused by the mixture of anger and longing it evoked. She slammed the book shut and put it back on the coffee table, where Maddie had strategically placed it.

When she looked at her mother's stomach, she thought of those photographs.

After breakfast, they drove downtown to McBee's. The escalator climbed through different departments on its way up to the sixth floor.

"I want to price the cribs later," Maddie said over her shoulder. "I could kick myself for giving yours away."

"Why did you?" Katie stepped aside to let a boy in a hurry climb past her.

"It seemed like something I wouldn't be needing again. You can never tell how things will change.

"Do you have any white dresses?" Maddie asked a saleswoman, who pointed brusquely to a rack by the wall.

With an experienced eye, Maddie flipped through the dresses, pulling one out every so often until she had four over her arm. "Let's start with these."

The first dress had a ruffled skirt and eyelet lace trim.

"Too frilly. Looks like a pinafore," Maddie said.

The next had a low-cut neckline and a fitted bodice.

"Scarlett O'Hara," Maddie joked.

The third was seersucker, with a scooped neck, tucks across the front, and deep, square pockets on the skirt, simple enough to wear all summer.

Katie put her hands in the pockets and twirled around. "I like it."

They weren't so lucky finding a dress for the dance. After McBee's, they tried the Village Tree and the Clothes Closet. Nothing pleased them both.

"I'm not a baby, Mom," Katie complained when her mother said a dress was too old.

"You're not a bar waitress, either."

"Forget it. I'll wear a skirt or something," Katie said, sulking.

"Don't be ridiculous. We'll find something. Let's try that shop on the other side of town, the one in that old yellow house."

As soon as they walked in, Katie spotted the dress, a deep-green cotton with tiny yellow flowers sprinkled lightly over it, draped over the back of a wicker rocker.

"It reminds me of Grandma's house, the fields along the cliff," Katie said in a rush of excitement.

The green dress fit. It was absolutely plain, with a square neckline and a sash that tied in the back.

"It shows off those lovely bones," Maddie said. She pointed to Katie's collarbones, and the little hollows they made.

In the car going home, Katie remembered Maddie's shape. Would it show at graduation? Everyone else's mother would look normal.

"What will you wear to graduation?" Katie asked.

"Something cool. It's usually so hot at those things. The purple smock, maybe. That's very light."

Katie groaned. "Do you have anything else?"

"Like what?"

"I don't know. There must be something that isn't so obvious."

"So obviously a maternity dress?"

Katie nodded glumly, caught between not wanting to discuss it and needing to make sure her mother wouldn't embarrass her. It was a shame to argue after Maddie had been so nice about the dresses.

Maddie frowned. "Honey, I'm not going to hide being pregnant." She struggled to keep the conversation light. "It's very fashionable these days, older women having babies."

Katie kept her eyes on the road.

Maddie sighed and shook her head. "You're a throwback. They used to make women hide inside until the baby was born." She turned to look at Katie directly for a moment; they had stopped for a light. "I'm sorry I embarrass you, but I intend to see you graduate and I'll wear what I please."

"Mom," Katie started, wanting to apologize, to cross the chasm that had opened between them, and recapture the morning's happy mood. But she faltered, not knowing what to say.

She felt the wall of Maddie's anger all the way home. After parking the car, her mother went upstairs without saying another word.

Katie ate lunch alone. Here they were, arguing. Back and forth, back and forth. Would it be like this all summer? It might even get worse when the baby came. She didn't know what to do.

Graduation

The graduation dance was more like a good-bye party than a dance. Everyone went, not just the popular kids or the kids who were already dating. Everyone. Even guys like Martin Henchill, who only talked to computers, and girls like Patsy Ryan, who still bought her clothes in the children's department.

"Katie, get your parents to come. Please? We're desperate," begged Allison, who was in charge of lining up the chaperons. "Your stepfather's cute. I'd love to get him out on the dance floor. Not really! This is serious. We're four chaperons short. If we can't come up with more, there might not be a dance."

Katie knew she was exaggerating. "You've asked everyone?"

"No. I skipped people like Mrs. Arthur. She always wants to organize the bunny hop, and stuff like that. I want to find people who will leave us alone."

"I'll think about it," Katie said. "But they're probably busy."

That wasn't true. She just didn't want them there. But what she wanted didn't count for much.

"Mrs. Ellis called me today and asked if Steve and I would chaperon the dance," Maddie told her at dinner.

"What did you say?"

"I said we'd be happy to. I haven't done anything for your class all year."

"You could've asked me first."

"That's true, but I didn't."

It was bad enough that they were going to be at graduation. At least there would be a big crowd there. But at the dance everyone would see them. Maddie in some dumb loose dress, and Steve who looked more like a high-school kid than a father-to-be. What if Allison really did ask him to dance?

"Don't be upset," Ruth said on the phone later. "My parents will be there, too. And they always insist on dancing, no matter how dumb it looks. They look ridiculous, especially my father. He looks like an elephant with an itch. Relax. Compared to my parents, yours look normal. Nobody will notice them."

On the night of the dance, Katie rode to school with Maddie and Steve, slunk down on the back seat chewing her lip. She hoped no one would see her with them.

As soon as they reached the door to the gym she mumbled, "Thanks for the ride," and hurried off to join a group of her friends. Glancing back, she saw Maddie and Steve holding hands, looking unsure of what to do next.

The gym bleachers were folded back to make room for tables with blue tablecloths and bouquets of yellow and white daisies. Crepe paper crisscrossed the walls and ceiling, and balloons hung in clumps, like models of the elements in science class. Along one side stood a line of tables for the buffet: fruit cup, lasagna, salad, cake. The parents helped serve.

"Having a good time?" Steve asked as he loaded salad onto Katie's plate.

"Uh-huh," she said softly, hoping the next person in line wouldn't guess they were related.

After dinner, the tables were pushed to the sides to make room for dancing. At first, the music played to an empty floor. Everyone stood in the corners and along the wall talking. Then a few couples ventured out, like scouts checking enemy territory. Finally, a fast song filled the floor with dancers in pairs and groups.

When a slow dance came next, someone turned the lights down. Jimmy Moran asked Katie to dance. He'd been her science partner all year. He put his arms around her waist and she hung hers loosely around his neck. Moving slowly, they swayed back and forth with their heads together.

Katie closed her eyes, lulled by the music. She'd known Jimmy since kindergarten. Last year, they'd had art together. Jimmy's clay castle had surpassed everyone else's. He'd added towers and spires, a hidden staircase, a moat, and a drawbridge, and even had made a dragon peering out over the tower wall. To surprise him, Katie had made a tiny princess and placed her at the castle's front door. Delighted, Jimmy had fired it along with the castle so it became a permanent part.

The music stopped.

"Good luck next year," Jimmy said.

"You, too."

He waved as he walked off to join his friends.

Katie started to look for her friends but stopped and sat by herself on the bleachers for a while, swinging her legs and watching the dancers. Even though she was having fun, she felt sad. Below, she could see her mother dancing with Steve. Ruth's parents were dancing, too. All around the gym, people were talking and laughing. Ian Summers was trying to catch Laura Forman, who was laughing so hard she was almost bent over double. Over by the tables, Ellen Todd and her group were still eating cake.

It's practically the last time we'll be together, Katie thought. She had never noticed an ending before. I'll never be in eighth grade again, she thought. I'll never skip recess and hide in the music room, never walk through the library making my favorite books stick out from the rest on the shelves.

"Hey, Katie, wanna dance?"

Rob Petrone lived at the end of her block. She slid down from her perch. She danced one dance after another with different people the rest of the evening, keeping a careful distance from Maddie and Steve. Before she realized it, the lights flicked on and off and Mr. Dodds, the principal, said, "Last dance, everyone." A slow record started. Katie was standing next to Rick Sanchez, a new boy. By midwinter, his English had improved enough to let the class discover what a natural clown he was.

"Let's dance," she said.

The floor was filled with the most unlikely couples. Tall Mona with tiny Eric. Rachel, who always studied, with Jake, who never did homework. A mix of old friends, new friends, people with crushes, and people who were just pals.

"Will you miss this school, Katie?"

"I guess so. It's silly, I know."

"Not silly to me. I miss my school in Puerto Rico still."

"Are you glad you came here?"

"Mostly glad. But I can be glad and sad at the same time."

"That's just how I feel."

They stopped talking and listened to the song as they danced. When it was over, the lights came up.

"I'll look for you next year at the high school," Rick said.

Maddie and Steve were waiting at the gym door. In the sky above the playground, the moon was almost full. It looked like a balloon from the dance—as if one had escaped from the gym and found a higher niche for itself. Katie tried to keep it in sight the whole trip home.

The morning of graduation was steaming, just as Maddie had predicted.

After lunch, Katie showered. Maddie had left her dress hanging on the bedroom door. She slipped it over her head, combed her hair, and put on some of the lipstick Maddie had put in her Christmas stocking, along with a set of jacks. "Something for both sides of you," she'd said.

Maddie was standing in the front hall when Katie came downstairs. "I don't feel old enough to have such a lovely daughter. I still feel about fifteen inside."

"You don't look fifteen, Mom." Katie gave her a gentle pat on her belly. "You look nice, though—really."

Maddie's dress had none of the frills, bows, or little collars that make maternity dresses look like oversize children's clothes.

"I'm glad you think so." Neither mentioned the argument on the shopping trip.

When Katie waved good-bye to Maddie and Steve at the school door, she was surprised by a rush of pride. They looked so happy standing together.

"We'll be front and center, the closest seats we can get," Maddie said.

"Good luck. You look terrific," Steve added.

Katie hurried in to find her place in line.

Graduation practice had seemed endless, standing for hours waiting her turn to walk down the center aisle, or standing in front of the folding chairs to practice sitting down in unison. Now, suddenly, the proud sound of the band filled the air, and the ceremony began.

The line moved down the aisle in time to the music. No one bumped the folding chairs. Once they were seated, Katie tried to find her father in the crowd. Maddie and Steve were right where they'd said they'd be, but there was no sign of her father's tall frame and red beard. Maybe he'd come late and was standing at the back, she thought.

Soon it was over. The class marched out to the band music, and once in the hall, they hugged, kissed, and slapped each other's backs, saying, "Congratulations," "That a way," and "All right!"

At the reception in the cafeteria, Katie found Maddie easily, but there was still no sign of Ed.

"I can't believe he missed this," Maddie said. "Typical."

Katie felt pulled between her own disappointment and an urge to defend her father.

"I'm sure there's a good reason," Steve said evenly. "Let's leave a message on the answering machine. Maybe he can meet us at the restaurant."

"We'd better get going. The reservation's for six," Maddie said.

Ed didn't show up at the restaurant, either. Somewhere between the shrimp cocktail and the lobster, Katie forgot to keep looking for him.

The telegram was waiting under the door when they got home.

"Sorry, baby. Assignment in Rome. I'll make it up in August. Love Dad."

Make it up in August? How? He was the one who'd missed something. He hadn't seen her graduate and walk down the aisle with her class. She crumpled the telegram and tossed it into the wastepaper basket by the hall table.

Summer Starts

The morning after graduation, Katie called Ruth after breakfast. "Let's go shopping for bathing suits."

"If we go now, we can still get to the pool after lunch," Ruth said. "I'm going to swim every day. That's my summer resolution. Maybe I can make the swim team in high school if I really practice."

Katie listened unenthusiastically. The swim team had to practice every morning. You could get pickled in all that chlorine. "I'll leave my bike at your house. We can take the bus."

She pulled on a pair of green running shorts, a striped polo shirt, and her old sneakers. In her knapsack she packed last year's suit, suntan lotion, and a copy of *Gone with the Wind.* She put her graduation money from her grandmother in her pocket. If she was lucky, there'd be enough for a bathing suit and new sandals, too. She thought it over and added some of her baby-sitting money.

Inside the store, a few shoppers walked the aisles. The girls went straight to the Junior section and began to flip through the rack of one-piece suits.

"I won't wear one with cups," said Ruth, holding up an example, a bright orange suit with hollow breasts pointing frontward.

Katie looked at it. "Barbie's the only one I've ever seen with boobs like that."

"Remember my sister's friend at the pool last summer? She was lying on her stomach, and when she rolled over, her bathing suit was dented," Ruth said.

Katie kept on sorting through the racks.

"Do you girls need help?" The saleswoman had a gruff voice, the hint of a mustache, and no trace of a smile.

"Not yet, we're still looking, thanks." Katie tried to be pleasant.

"Three suits at a time in the dressing room." The saleswoman waddled off, a tank on patrol.

"They always act like you're trying to shoplift, you know? It's insulting. She wouldn't act like that if our mothers were with us," Ruth said.

Each girl brought three suits to the large dressing room.

"You're supposed to leave your underpants on so you don't catch a disease," Ruth said.

"Or spread one," Katie teased.

They made several trips back to the rack, and each tried on at least ten suits before she found the one she liked. Cut like a racing suit, with shiny purple, yellow, green, and pink stripes as narrow as pencil lines, Katie's suit gleamed as if it were wet. Ruth's was striped, too: blue and white with red trim.

"Looks like something Shirley Temple would wear on the 'Good Ship *Lollipop*,'" Katie teased. "No, no. I'm only kidding," she added as Ruth punched her in the arm. "Be careful! I'll get a bruise and look worse in my suit."

"Impossible! Come on, let's go. I want to get to the pool early," said Ruth. "There's a new lifeguard up by the diving area. I want to put my towel near him."

Katie nodded. Nothing new. Ruth had a crush. Summer had just started, but she never lost time. So that was why she was going to swim every day.

The guard had freckles. He looked more like somebody's older brother than a movie-star type. Ruth managed to find a spot for their towels close to his chair. She sat on the edge of the pool, dangling her legs in the water and talking easily, as if every day she made small talk with an older guy.

Katie lay on her stomach a few feet away, trying to read but distracted by their conversation. How does she know what to say? Isn't she afraid he'll guess she likes him? They were talking about dogs. Ruth's family had a shaggy tan mutt named Sandman, who loved to sleep. When they were little, Katie and Ruth used to sprawl next to Sandman and use him for a pillow as they read. Ruth was describing Sandman's dreams, how he ran in his sleep, legs jerking as he lay on his side, little yelps coming from deep in his throat.

How can she talk to him so smoothly? I'd be fumbling for words, maybe even stuttering, Katie thought. Ruth coolly tossed her braid over her shoulder. Panic crawled down Katie's spine. *What if Ruth starts dating? What if she starts really going out a lot?* Katie propped her chin on her folded arms and watched Ruth and the guard. *I'll be stuck at home. I don't want to hang around Mom and Steve. Maybe I'll get a lot of baby-sitting jobs. Make tons of money. And I'll be at Grandma's in August with Dad.* She shrugged. *He hasn't even asked her out yet.*

Even so, Katie had the same stranded, lonely feeling she got at home lately.

She went back to reading her book. The passions of Scarlett and Rhett were less troubling than Ruth's love life. Katie didn't look up again until a shower of tiny drops hit her shoulders. Ruth stood over her, hands outstretched like a sorceress casting a spell. She wiped her hands on a towel and sat down cross-legged.

"He's cute," Katie said.

Ruth nodded glumly.

"What's wrong? I thought the conversation was going fine."

"It was. Then this high-school girl butted in. 'Oh, hi, Jimmy. I didn't know you were working here.'" Ruth exaggerated a high-pitched, sweet voice. "She's in his class in high school. Everything on her body is pink. Even her sunglasses. Pink with ruffles. I couldn't believe it. As soon as she showed up, our conversation fizzled."

"Pink-ruffled sunglasses?"

"No, dummy. Just pink plastic. The ruffles were on her bikini." Ruth flopped over on her stomach. "It's okay," she sighed. "It's fun just to try it out. Talking to older guys. Got to get ready for the fall, right?"

Katie nodded, but she didn't agree. She wasn't even

ready to try. Talking to boys in her class was hard enough sometimes. She leaned her cheek against her towel and felt the heat from the concrete seep in. It was relaxing, comforting, like the heating pad her mother gave her when she had cramps.

She'd only had them twice, but the pain had a grip that threatened to hold on forever. Her mother had settled Katie on the couch in the living room with a pillow and the plaid blanket from Scotland and brought her a cup of spice tea. Then she plugged in the quilted satin heating pad. "Tuck this right in by your stomach. The heat will relax those muscles. They're just not used to it yet." Katie remembered snuggling under the blanket, closing her eyes, and feeling the steady heat from the pad penetrate her body. Slowly the pain let go its hold.

As she lay by the pool, the concrete warmed her body and eased the thought of Ruth leaving her behind. She fell asleep and woke up when Ruth jostled her shoulder and said, "Come on. It's after four. My mother wants to go over the job with us."

Katie stretched and yawned. Her skin felt tight. The sun was mild now, its midday heat calmed to a comfortable glow. Little boys with plastered hair did cannonballs off the board. The guard watched halfheartedly. His pink-ruffled friend had disappeared. There was another hour to go before closing.

Katie and Ruth cycled home through air fresh with the smell of new-mown grass. Every boy in town with a summer gardening job must have started today. Overhead, thick-leafed trees touched above the street, making tunnels of green light. They passed hopscotch, jump-rope, and kickball games. An ice-cream truck repeated its tinkly re-frain over and over again. The streets were filled with a sense of summer's beginning and its limitless possibilities.

Mrs. Ives was sitting on the porch in an old wicker chair. Her eyes were closed. For a minute the girls thought she was asleep, but she smiled when she heard their steps on the creaky porch stairs.

"Oh, good, you remembered," she said. "I was just sitting here enjoying the sounds. It's like a little symphony: birds, bicycle bells, sprinkler water hitting the leaves, someone's piano, the ice-cream truck—all these light, musical sounds. And the smells! Grass, roses, mint, pine. You never notice it until you sit down."

Ruth rolled her eyes. Mrs. Ives noticed and laughed. She knew her ramblings embarrassed her children, but she didn't mind. "It's your limitation, not mine," she always told them.

"Let's take a look at the rooms," she said. "Don't panic. Rooms always look worse when they're not lived in. There's lots to do, but with the three of us working, it will go fast."

"Steve knows a lot about this. He said he'd show us some techniques," Katie said.

"Good!" said Mrs. Ives. "That will be a big help."

"I'll ask him when he comes home. Maybe he can show us tomorrow. He usually can take off early from work."

"Lucky man," said Mrs. Ives.

Steve came home from work at three the next day and took Katie and Ruth to a hardware store in the next town. He picked out rubber gloves, three types of steel wool, sandpaper, and a big can of paint remover.

At the house, Mrs. Ives explained her plans. Steve ran his fingers over the woodwork.

"There's at least two layers of paint here. Let's try some paint remover and see how it goes."

He showed them how to brush on the thick pink liquid, wait for it to loosen the layers of old paint, then take it off with paint scrapers and steel wool.

The biting smell from the paint remover stung Katie's eyes and nose.

"Try this," said Mrs. Ives, handing her a paper mask for her nose and mouth. She opened the windows wide to let in as much air as possible.

They started on the job for real the following Monday. The trick was to alternate. Paint the remover on one section, strip another in the meantime. When you got a rhythm going, you didn't have to wait. But soon Katie's arms began to ache from scraping and her knees hurt from the hard floor. She heard Ruth groan.

"This is boring! My back aches."

"My arms do, too," Katie said. "How long have we been working?"

"Only half an hour. Would you believe it?"

Katie shook her head and went back to scraping. The flat parts went fairly fast, but the curves and corners in the molding were tough. The paint stuck in every crack and seam. "This is harder than I thought it would be," she said.

By noon, each girl had finished scraping one window. They packed sandwiches and headed for the pool again, happy to be far away from the noxious smell of the pink goo.

Prickly Heat

Summer went smoothly at first. The job got easier. Steve gave the girls more tips on scraping. Katie worked with him in the garden, too, weeding, watering, and planting more seeds. Maddie and Katie hadn't argued since the shopping trip. Katie was out of the house most of the time. But in mid-July, a heat wave clamped down on the town and didn't budge for more than a week. Temperatures stayed above ninety, climbing to a hundred by noon. In the still evenings you could hear the hum of air conditioners working.

"Too hot to move," said Maddie, patting her swelling belly. "Now I know why hippos lie in the river all day. Creatures of bulk can't take the heat. I'd lie in the water all day, too, if I could."

On the fourth day of the heat wave, Maddie was setting things out for dinner when Katie got home. "Feels good here," she said, standing in front of the open refrigerator. She was barefoot and her hair was piled up on top of her head in a little knot. She paused to wipe perspiration off her forehead.

"I'm making a chef's salad. Give me a hand?" Maddie put tomatoes, green peppers, and a zucchini on the table. "The paring knife is by the sink."

Katie had just come in from hanging her bathing suit on the line. The pool had been bathwater-warm and crowded. Someone had stolen her plastic bracelets from her towel while she was in the water.

"Do this, do that. All I ever do is work around here," she grumbled as she got out the chopping board. She was half joking, half serious.

Maddie snorted, "Are you kidding? Asking you to make your bed is a major deal." She sounded half joking, half serious, too.

Katie chopped for a while before answering. I do a lot, she told herself. "I empty the dishwasher," she pointed out. "And I clean the cat box."

"He's your cat."

"I vacuumed the stairs last week."

"Okay. Once. That's not much." Maddie sighed. "Katie, I didn't start this, but since you did, I'll tell you. You really *don't* do so much. You play music, talk on the phone, and drape yourself on the couch reading. You rarely ask if you can help. Maybe Steve's right—I have spoiled you."

Katie could imagine them discussing her. Now she felt really angry.

52:

"That's what Steve says? If he doesn't like it around here, why'd he have to come?"

"You sound like a six-year-old. We're just concerned about your attitude, that's all."

Katie felt as sullen as the weather. "Why should I have a good attitude? Nobody asked me if I wanted Steve here. Now the baby coming. Big deal. The happy little family."

For a moment the kitchen was silent. A fly buzzed against the window screen.

"Wait just a minute. Do I hear you correctly? Nobody asked you if you wanted Steve to come? Who are you, the queen?"

Katie stared out the window, embarrassed. How had they ever got into this argument?

Maddie continued. "I didn't have to ask you if I could marry Steve. I didn't need permission."

She paused again, as if searching for words, and studied Katie's face. Her voice grew softer. "Katie, you've made it harder than it has to be. We want you in this family, but sometimes it seems as if you're deliberately building a wall."

Katie finished chopping the pepper and scraped the little pieces into the salad bowl. She knew Maddie was watching her. "Can I go now?" she asked sarcastically. She kept her eyes away from her mother's face.

The room was silent. Katie stared out the window. She didn't dare to blink, for fear that tears might spill over and give her away.

"I'll leave the salad in the fridge," Maddie said at last. "Eat when you want to."

Katie slammed the kitchen door behind her. She stayed in her room until after dark, leafing through old magazines. She could hear Maddie and Steve eating dinner on the porch.

Much later, when the door to the front bedroom closed, she tiptoed down to the kitchen and made a peanut-butter sandwich. Then she sat on the front porch swing, her arms wrapped around her legs and her chin resting on her knees.

The heat hadn't broken, but she felt a chill. Had she really built a wall? It was easier to think of Maddie and Steve as the ones who had pushed her out.

Maybe I can live with Dad. I could cook for him, she thought. And do the laundry. When I visit, I'll show him. I'll make lasagna and mint-fudge brownies with chocolate chips. I'll do the dishes. I'll prove I'm indispensable. I could go to school in the city and have all new friends.

But what if he has a girlfriend?

The idea brought her fantasy to a stop.

If he has a girlfriend, she won't want me around. She probably makes her own brownies.

She felt tired. Other questions would have to wait. She locked the front door behind her and climbed the stairs in the dark. She undressed quickly and slid in between fresh, smooth sheets, different from the wrinkled ones she'd climbed out of in the morning. Mom must have changed them, she thought.

A Phone Call from Ed

After the argument, Maddie and Katie circled each other like wary cats. The heat continued.

When Katie was little, Ed had told her stories every night. She remembered them during the hot nights after the fight. Ed used to sprawl at the foot of her bed, his long legs resting on the floor, crossed at the ankles, his hands folded behind his head. Sometimes the stories were about her. Katie the circus girl. Katie the ballerina. Because he was a photographer, he was especially good at details. Katie could still remember her circus outfit, blue-green with shining silver trim, like waves breaking in the moonlight.

Sometimes the stories were about Louie Lookout, a six-inch-tall man. He had to look out for dangers like little children's grabby fingers. Elaine, a large black beetle, gave him rides on her back. Elaine liked to dance and would stand up on her back legs, swaying her big shell from side to side.

Katie wanted Ed to make Louie marry Elaine. But Ed said no, Louie wasn't a marrying man. He needed to be on the lookout. He couldn't settle down. It wouldn't be in character.

Now that Katie thought about it, Louis Lookout seemed a lot like Ed.

Katie hadn't thought of Ed's stories in years. What made her remember them this summer?

Ed called the third week of July to discuss her visit. Usually they went together to his mother's beach house for most of August. But this spring Grandma had been sick.

"I don't want to tire her out. So I thought we'd go down for a weekend, but stay in town the rest of the time. It's great in the summer, Katie. Music outside. Lots of people and food everywhere. I think you'll like it."

Katie felt a tug of longing for the familiar beach house, where nothing ever changed. The same rattan furniture with flowered cushions had been on the porch since her father was a child. Maybe since Grandma was a child, Katie thought. The same books and toys were on the shelves, no matter how many cousins had come and gone. And the same sharp salt smell blew in the windows day and night.

Grandma always seemed the same, too. Her short gray hair framed her head in a springy halo. She was tall and bony, and her long, thin feet were always encased in faded sneakers. She wore khaki shorts or chino pants and old shirts that once belonged to Grandpa. When he was alive, they had used the beach house only on weekends. But now that she was alone, Grandma lived there the year round.

"I watch the seasons blow in and out here. It gives me the illusion that I can see time passing by. It's reassuring at my age," she said.

Katie found it hard to imagine Grandma being sick. She seemed invincible, but that had to do with her spirit, not with her body. Grandma would take illness as a personal insult.

"Maybe Grandma will feel better by next month," she said to Ed.

"If she is, we'll stay a few days longer."

That relieved her. This summer, more than ever, she wanted things to stay the same.

Leaving for Ed's

Katie left for Ed's at the beginning of August. She and Ruth had finished scraping and painting. Katie decided that she'd never do it for a living, but the final result was beautiful.

The soft blue and yellow Ruth's grandmother had chosen made the rooms look larger. The oiled woodwork was a warm tan, and plain white curtains hung from brass rods at the windows. Mrs. Ives had moved in a few pieces of furniture: a small sofa, a white wicker table, a rocker, and a standing lamp with a tulip glass shade filled the living room. The bedroom held a single bed, a night table, an oak dresser with a round mirror above it, and a chair with a cane seat. The effect was spare but graceful.

"Your grandmother will love it," Katie told Ruth. "Anyone would."

"Mom's worried. I heard her telling my father. She's afraid Granny will be unhappy, especially with all us kids around."

"I thought that was the whole idea. Company, conversation—right?"

"But Granny's never stayed here for long. She's used to a big, fancy apartment. Next to that, this might seem pretty crummy."

Katie looked at the rooms again. "Well, if she doesn't want this, I'll move in, okay?"

Mrs. Ives came in with her checkbook. "Katie, talk to my children first. They're always threatening to move out." She paused to write two checks. "Here, that should float your city spending spree, Katie, and Ruth, you can put this toward that tape deck."

They rode downtown right away. Ruth deposited her check in her savings account. Katie got traveler's checks. Then they went to Jack's for sodas.

"I doubt if I'll spend much of it," Katie said.

"You might see something really great. I wish I were coming! Are you scared?"

Katie nodded. "A little. Mom's always come with me before. Even when I went into the city for dinner with Dad, she came with me on the train and met me afterward. This time I'm completely on my own."

"What will I do, stuck here the whole month?" Ruth complained.

"Keep working on that guard."

"He's hopeless. I've given up."

"Come on. You never give up."

Ruth grinned. Katie was right. In seventh grade, Ruth had had a crush on an eighth-grader named Terry Swann. All year long she'd made conversation—at the bus stop, in the cafeteria, at the library. "How's the ravioli?" "Nice shot in the basketball game." That spring, he invited her to an eighth-grade graduation party. She'd been the only seventh-grader there.

"Okay, I haven't give up. But he's not interested. I saw him at the movies with a girl. I bet he's going with her."

"Maybe it was his sister."

"He was holding her hand."

"Maybe it was his mother. Were they crossing a street?"

Ruth laughed. "No. They were sitting in the balcony. She looked about sixteen."

"Not his mother, huh?"

"No. Definitely not. Anyway, I'd rather go with you. We should've asked your father."

Katie nodded, but she knew she had to go alone. That was the only way she'd find out about living with Ed.

"Well, at least bring me a souvenir," Ruth said. "I'll miss you."

Maddie took off from work to drive Katie to the train. In the car, Katie sat quietly, staring blankly out the window.

"Nervous?" Maddie asked.

"A little." It wasn't the train ride or the city. It was Ed. She hadn't spent much time with him in the past year. Before, when she saw him at Grandma's, or met him for a day, he had been like a pal. They had played together, in a way. Visits to the zoo, the carousel, the circus. But those things wouldn't fit this year. She was older. She didn't know what she wanted him to do or be like this time. She had vague notions of the two of them walking through a museum together, or eating dinner at a restaurant with little tables and checkered tablecloths. But how would he know she'd changed? The postcard he'd sent from Paris had had a picture of some children sailing boats in a fountain. And when he came back from Mexico he'd brought her a piñata. She would have preferred a peasant blouse. But she wasn't going to tell Maddie all this. She shrugged instead.

Maddie patted her hand. "Call me if anything goes wrong. Any time. Even if you're just homesick or blue. And you can come home any time. Ed will understand."

For a moment, Katie wanted to bury her head in her mother's lap and let the tears flow out, all the hot, angry tears. She wanted to go back to a time when she'd kept no secrets from her. She wanted to have Maddie make it all better. But Maddie's belly, beginning to bulge with the baby, filled her lap.

"I'll be okay," Katie said.

She pulled her suitcase from the back seat and carried it to the platform as the train pulled in.

"Have fun, sweetheart." Maddie kissed her. "Call me tonight."

Katie found a seat by the window and sat down just as the train started to roll. She waved to her mother.

As the train picked up speed, she watched landmarks roll by. The playground with the slide where she'd cut her head. The church where her Brownie troop used to meet. The pond where she'd learned to skate. The clock tower of the high school. The green of the park. Then the town was gone, left behind her as the train rumbled toward the city.

In the City

Ed stood underneath the big clock, just as he had promised, his red hair visible above the tops of people's heads. He grinned and waved when he saw Katie.

"Look at you! Dream Angel," he teased, quoting rock and roll as he often did. "When did you get so old?" He squeezed her close in a hug. "Hungry? Let's get out of here and grab some food. There's a great Chinese place near the house."

Holding her suitcase with one hand, he led her through the crowd of weary commuters, talking over his shoulder.

"Baby, you don't know how good you look. Like sunshine on a cloudy day. Remember 'My Girl'?"

"Sure. The Temptations." It was a game they always played, rock-and-roll quizzes.

62:

"Good! Hey, I'm sorry I missed your graduation. Couldn't be helped. Was Maddie mad?" He shrugged, not waiting for an answer. "Here's our bus."

Ed zigzagged past people bunched at the front of the bus to get seats in the back. Katie looked out at the store windows. As they moved uptown, the traffic thinned and the bus moved faster.

Ed pulled the signal cord, and the bus pulled over at the next corner. Katie followed her father past brick buildings that were all alike, with rounded fronts and wide stone steps. He held her hand at corners. Even though it felt strange, she didn't pull away.

Afternoon sun, reflected off the mirror over the mantel, filled Ed's apartment.

"Here it is—home for the week."

The space and neatness took Katie by surprise. She'd visited the apartment only once or twice before and hadn't noticed its appearance. Healthy plants hung in the bay window. Imagine Ed taking care of plants, Katie thought. Maybe he and Steve had more in common than she thought.

Ed led her to a small room off the living room. "This is my office. This week it's all yours. I was going to put you on the couch, but kids your age need privacy, right?"

Ed had pushed his desk into one corner and set up a folding cot against the wall. He'd moved an old trunk in front of the window as a night table, and clamped a reading light to a shelf above the cot.

"I cleared out the top drawer of the file. And the top of the desk's all yours."

While Ed made a call, Katie sat cross-legged on the cot, enjoying the little room, snug as a ship's cabin. He really thought about how I'd feel while I'm here, Katie realized. The idea jarred her image of Ed, careless, joking, and forgetful. Above the desk hung shelves filled with books, journals, albums, and a corkboard with pictures and postcards stuck on haphazardly. Katie eyed the pictures. Several showed women.

She had never met Ed's girlfriends. Once he'd brought a woman with him to Grandma's. She'd worn a man's sleeveless undershirt belted with a sash, and through the thin fabric, wings of shoulder blades sprang from her back. She had seemed more child than woman. But she wasn't his girlfriend after all, just another photographer working with him on a project. All afternoon they had discussed layouts while Katie sat beside them on the beach reading and letting the sand dribble through her fingers. Maybe I'll meet his girlfriend this time, Katie thought.

"All set?" Ed asked, poking his head through the door.

Katie smoothed her skirt, straightened her sandal straps, and followed her father downstairs. The restaurant was a few blocks uptown. They walked past a fruit market, a bookstore, a bakery, several shoe stores ("Don't ask me why there are so many," Ed said), and a supermarket. The air was layered with smells: coffee grounds, garbage, fresh bread, dog poop, cookies, flowers, and stale, damp subway air that blew out of vents in the street. Wilted people passed on the sidewalk, clothes wrinkled and damp with sweat. Everyone was heading home to showers, air-conditioning, and cold drinks.

"Here it is." Ed opened the door to a small Chinese restaurant.

He picked a booth near the front window. "Try the sesame noodles," he told her. "They're spicy. And we'll get some mu shu pork with pancakes, and the strange-tasting chicken. That's its name, honest."

Ed gave the order to the waiter, who brought tea and ice water to the table.

"So how've you been?"

"Okay. Busy." She shrugged awkwardly.

"Busy doing what?"

"Ruth and I fixed up some rooms in the Iveses' house. We took all the paint off the woodwork."

"That's hard work! Paint remover stinks, doesn't it?"

"It gave us headaches at first. Steve showed us how to do it and made sure we used rubber gloves." Embarrassed at mentioning Steve, she glanced at her father to see his reaction. He was pouring tea.

"So what else have you been doing?"

"I went to the pool every day with Ruth. We planted a vegetable garden behind our house, and I weeded it a lot." She avoided mentioning Steve's name this time. She couldn't think of anything else to say. My life is pretty boring, she thought.

The garden interested Ed. "I thought about putting a garden there but never got around to it."

That's what Mom said, Katie thought.

Ed signaled the waiter for more tea. "There's a lot we can do this week. Movies, museums. What do you think you'd like?"

"Everything, I guess." She felt so dumb.

Just then the waiter brought the dinner.

"Have I told you about my trip to Alaska?" Ed said. "It was amazing. Huge mountains, much bigger than anything on this coast. And the glaciers!"

All Katie had to do was listen. Thank goodness. Her

chopsticks crisscrossed awkwardly until Ed showed her how to hold them. She tried it his way and it worked.

"Grandma's feeling much better," Ed said as the waiter brought the check. "She probably could have handled us coming for the week, but I'm glad we have these days together. We'll go down to the beach Friday for a long weekend."

After dinner, they walked through the park. People were playing softball and tennis, throwing Frisbees, lying on picnic blankets, sitting on benches.

"So tomorrow we'll go downtown to a museum. Maybe get tickets to a play." Ed rattled off plans as they walked.

Katie's stomach ached from all the food. Her head ached, too. By the time they reached the apartment, she was longing for a shower and some time alone.

After showering, she kissed her father goodnight.

"Dad, remember Louis Lookout?" Katie asked.

Ed nodded. "I haven't thought of him in a long time."

"I wonder what happened to him."

"Maybe he married that beetle after all," Ed said with a wink.

"I doubt it," Katie said. "Remember, he's not the marrying type."

"People change, you know," Ed said.

Lying in the little room, Katie tried to read, but after a few minutes she turned off the lamp and lay on her back, looking out the window. She could see the yellow squares of windows in the buildings across the street. Cars swooshed past below, and a few streets away an ambulance siren whined.

Why did she feel so awkward? She didn't know what to

say to him. Her answers sounded short, maybe even rude. There was nothing she could tell him that was really worth hearing about. It was all dumb stuff—going to the pool, riding bikes, hanging around with Ruth, playing tennis on the high-school courts.

It was easier at Grandma's. There was so much space— big, cool rooms to sit and read in, the porch for rocking. You didn't always have to talk. You could do things instead. And Grandma helped, too. She asked Ed about his work, or talked about books they both had read. She'd tell Katie funny stories about when Ed was a boy. It was easier with the three of them. But this week, it was going to be just the two of them. All week.

Jazz and a Change of Plans

"Up and at 'em," Ed sang into the little room.

Katie woke from a sound sleep. Sun bounced off every surface of the little room, and street noise ricocheted off the walls. She rubbed her eyes. What a shock! Like coming from a quiet, dark room into a loud party going full tilt. It was already hot. She put on her lightest sundress.

Ed had poured tall glasses of fresh orange juice. He stopped whistling to give her a kiss on the cheek.

"Sleep okay?"

She nodded.

"I'm making lemon pancakes. There's iced coffee in the refrigerator." He noticed her surprise. "Didn't think I could cook?"

Not cook, or clean, or even water plants. She'd imagined him living in a messy, crowded place with cans of film and beer in the refrigerator and dead plants gathering dust on the windowsill. She didn't dare to tell him.

"I know what you thought," he said. "Just because a man dresses informally doesn't mean he lives like a bum. You women! Think you're the only ones who know how to keep house." He shook his head wearily, but his eyes gave his joking away. "It's supposed to top ninety-five today. Let's take a boat trip around the harbor."

That was Ed, always changing plans. Unreliable, Maddie would have said. She liked to know things were set in advance. More interesting this way, was Ed's reply.

They found seats on the boat's top deck and sat side by side enjoying the sun and the breeze off the water. Every so often, Ed would snap a picture of Katie. Usually she didn't notice until the shutter clicked. He took pictures of other people, too: a lady in a frilly pink hat; an elderly couple dressed up—the man in a straw hat, the woman with a parasol; a tall, thin black man in a sheer white shirt.

Everywhere they went all week, Ed brought his camera. He took a few shots every day, sometimes of people, but also of things that caught his eye—a building that was half torn down, a row of telephone booths, all full. You couldn't predict what would interest him.

Katie's awkward feeling came and went. As the days passed, she found she could at least talk about things they'd just seen or done.

On Monday, Ed took her to hear a jazz group in a nightclub. A woman named Claire joined them there. She kissed Ed on the lips when she got to their table, and shook hands with Katie when introduced. Her smile and laugh put Katie at ease, and she found herself talking easily about school, books she liked, things she did with Ruth.

"I had a friend like that in eighth grade," Claire said. "We did everything together. We used to tell people we were sisters, and they believed us."

It was easy to imagine Claire back in eighth grade. She didn't act fancy or sophisticated, even though she was a grown woman. Katie liked her so much that it wasn't until later that she wondered exactly what Claire was to Ed, just a friend or someone special?

Katie had never listened to jazz before. At first the sounds seemed to jar against each other, stopping and starting abruptly, going off in all directions. She couldn't follow it. Then she noticed that sometimes the instruments took turns, with one in the forefront and the other two backing it up. She caught one short tune and listened to them toss it back and forth, changing it a little each time. Then she forgot about following and just let the music fill the room, feeling the excitement build up, crash and build again. She forgot her father and Claire. She sat all alone in the smoky room watching the figures lit by spots. Then the music stopped and applause poured out, bringing her back to the present.

Ed was watching her with a smile. "Another fan in the family," he said.

"It's great," she said, but the words were shallow. She couldn't begin to say how it had felt. Watching her father nod slowly, she knew she didn't have to explain.

She didn't bother trying to talk on the way home. She wanted to keep the feeling of the music in her head a little longer. It was still there when she fell asleep.

70:

She woke up just before sunrise. Pale purple light softened the room. She lay half-asleep, wondering why she'd woken up at all. Then she felt it, a sticky wetness on the insides of her thighs. Turning on the reading lamp above the bed, she saw the trickle of blood running down her leg and the brown stain on the sheet.

Not now, not here, she thought. She'd had her period before but it didn't come regularly yet and in the anticipation of the trip she'd forgotten it completely. I didn't bring anything. If I were home, I'd just tell Mom, but not Dad. How can I tell him? He'll know when he sees the sheets.

She lay in bed a few more minutes wishing it would go away. Just stop and disappear. Tears spilled down into her hair. Think! she told herself. Stop being a baby and think!

She grabbed a pair of underpants and headed for the bathroom, hoping Ed wouldn't hear her. She washed off her legs and then sat on the toilet trying to decide what to do. In the morning I'll go to a drugstore. But what about now? What about the sheet? She didn't want Ed to see the stain. It was too personal. You could talk to your mother about your period, but not to your father.

I can use toilet paper for now, she thought. She carefully folded it into a makeshift pad and fitted it into her underpants. That left only the sheet.

Tiptoeing back to the room, she pulled the sheet off the bed and carried it back to the bathroom. The blood came out with soap and cold water. Twisting it again and again, she wrung it as dry as she could. Then, tiptoeing back, she draped it over the desk chair, tucked the top sheet around the mattress, and lay down. Morning sounds rumbled already in the street, but Katie fell asleep anyway, relieved to have thought of a solution.

The next day, Ed didn't ask any questions when she went down to the corner drugstore. Things always seem worse at night than in the daytime, she decided.

They visited one museum in the morning and another after lunch. The first, once a millionaire's mansion, was paved with marble and dimly lit. In its cool rooms, elegant paintings hung.

The second was modern, with white walls and bright lights. The art on display vibrated with primary colors like the paintings of little children.

"Quite a change?" Ed said. "Which do you like?"

"Both, I guess. They're just different. The morning paintings were peaceful, but these are kind of like a circus."

Ed nodded. He pointed to a huge tricolor canvas on the wall. "The guys who make these haywire pictures live in the same crazy world that we do. Circus is a good word for it."

When they were out on the street again, Ed said, "Time to show you one of my favorite places. It's all photography. Wait till you see it. You're surrounded by images, all incredible."

From the outside, the store looked impossibly narrow. But after a skinny hall, it opened into a wide room. The far end was lined with books. The rest of the space held racks of cards and bins of posters and mounted prints.

Katie and Ed browsed through the card racks. Ed let her look without commenting.

Some images had an immediate beauty that reached out to her. A shell with a smooth, perfect curve; the moon rising over a tiny town; two lilies, white against a dark background. Others grabbed her with their harshness, disturbing her. An Appalachian family staring from a rickety doorway; strange twin girls, identical but oddly distinct in their velvet party dresses; black mine workers glistening with sweat.

"Pick out any you like," Ed said.

Katie chose twelve, in all. Some were beautiful, some scary, some hard to understand.

Ed whistled as he looked through her choices. "Minor White, Diane Arbus, Walker Evans, Cartier-Bresson. Phew! You've got taste, kid. You picked the greats."

Katie grinned at the compliment, but later, on the bus home, she wondered if there were any cards there that Ed wouldn't have approved of. Maybe she'd picked good photographs because that's all there were.

"Were there any pictures in the store that you didn't like?" she asked.

"What?"

"Were there any bad pictures in the store?"

"I don't like the fancy angles or distortion. It seems like trick photography to me. I like a clear, straight image, and I like people pictures more than objects. But that's just my taste. Bad pictures? Like cards with kittens and flowers?" He shook his head.

That night they ate dinner sitting on the floor at a Japanese restaurant.

On Wednesday morning, Ed's phone rang, and he stayed on for a long time talking business. He and Katie went to a play that afternoon. Ed didn't mention the call until dinner.

"Another change in plans," he told her. "It's an assignment on the Coast that I don't want to miss. I'm going to send you to Grandma's by yourself. I've got to leave tomorrow morning. I know it's short notice, but that's the way it works. Wherever the action is, you've got to hop. You don't mind, do you?"

Katie nodded, feeling like a doll with a bobbing head that sits in the back of a car window. What else could she say? No, don't go?

"Oh, good." He sighed. "I knew you'd understand. Here's what I thought. Instead of going right to your grandmother's tomorrow, you could stay in the city until Friday just like we'd planned. Claire will come and stay over with you. She's gotten hold of some tickets for the Center City Dancers—classical, modern, African, boogie-woogie, all mixed together. We thought since you liked the jazz so much, you'd enjoy it. What do you say?"

"It's just for one night, right?"

Ed nodded. "Right. I told her to take good care of my baby."

Was that a rock and roll quote? Katie wasn't sure, but she didn't want him to change the subject. "Is it okay with Grandma that I come by myself?"

"Fine with her. If my feelings weren't so tender, I'd admit that she'd rather have you all to herself. She says she's fully recovered. Wants you to stay longer—at least a week, maybe two. It's up to you. Think it over." He changed the subject abruptly. "Okay—who sings 'Stop in the Name of Love'?"

"Supremes."

"Very good."

"But I didn't bring enough stuff."

"I figured that, so I called Maddie. She said she'd mail some clothes to Grandma's so you'd have enough. You should call her when we get home and tell her what you want."

It would be good to talk to Maddie. Hearing her voice would make Katie feel rooted again.

At Ed's she felt as if she were sitting on the sidelines of his life. The more she watched him, the more she knew for certain that he wouldn't want her to live here. He liked to come and go with no one to worry about.

Ed left Thursday morning carrying a duffel full of clothes and a bag of camera equipment. Claire had come for breakfast. She and Katie washed up the dishes together after Ed took a taxi to the airport.

"We've got the whole day," Claire said. "Did you ever shop for clothes in secondhand stores? Some people call them antique clothes, but most of them aren't that old. It's fun. We can work our way downtown. You might find something you really like."

Katie agreed to try it. The first store, a tiny place named "Flora's," smelled like someone's musty attic. Katie wrinkled her nose. It wasn't the smell of perspiration, but it suggested other people, other times.

"Ignore it," Claire said. "It goes away as soon as you wash things or have them cleaned. You'll get used to it today, I bet."

Katie did, just as she got used to rows of old shoes and boxes of dusty postcards. To her, the clothes looked impossibly baggy and wrinkled. But Claire could spot hidden treasures on the racks: a black jacket with padded shoulders and a narrow waist made Katie look sophisticated; a white blouse with a square lace collor and full sleeves made her look elegant and innocent at the same time;

tweed trousers with pleats; a wine-colored wool skirt swirled as she walked.

They found other things, too: old postcards for Katie to send home; a man's straw hat to wear at the beach; chunky fake jewelry for laughs; a flowered tin box that Ruth would love.

Claire always tried on the evening gowns, slinky with jet embroidery and low-cut backs, made of chiffon or tiers of lace. Katie tried on a feather boa in one shop and a fur cape in another.

They giggled together, pulling things out for each other to see. Claire seemed genuinely glad to be with her and interested in what she had to say. Katie found herself telling her things she hadn't told anyone else.

As they sat eating lunch, she described Maddie and Steve, and struggled to explain the lonely feeling she had when they were acting close or loving.

Claire listened, sympathy and pain mixed on her face.

"I think I know exactly what you mean," Claire said. "I remember this time, not too long ago, before I met Ed, when my old roommate, Janet, fell in love. I mean really *FELL IN LOVE* overnight, whammo, with this man, Tom. They were my friends. But suddenly they were together and I was on the outside. Just watching them reminded me that I wasn't with anyone. Sometimes I had to leave because I thought I'd cry. It just made me sad, that's all. I can't explain it, really."

Katie nodded. She understood exactly. "My mom said, 'Can't you be happy for us?' I am happy for them but I'm sad inside at the same time. That's the main thing. Not all the time. But a lot of the time."

Tomorrow, I'll be at Gran's, Katie thought. Maybe I'll never see Claire again. Even though we've talked like this, I might not see her.

As if she could read her mind, Claire said, "I hope we keep in touch, Katie."

"Me, too."

"Good. Then, between us, we'll make sure it happens. Ed's wonderful but he's not what you'd call the marrying type."

Embarrassment made Katie shiver. Claire was definitely Ed's girlfriend. She knew the apartment so well, knew where the plates and silverware went. She moved around the living room straightening things almost as if they were hers.

"How do you know?"

Claire laughed and shook her head. She seemed to be laughing at herself. "He likes his life the way it is. Maybe some other time, later, he'll be interested in settling down. But for now, I doubt it. Don't worry, I'm pretty independent myself."

"I used to imagine coming to live with him," Katie confessed. "I had this daydream about how great it would be. I'd cook and stuff. I thought he needed that sort of thing." She sighed and shrugged her shoulders, trying to look nonchalant.

Claire reached across the table and took hold of Katie's hand. "Honey, he does need you. Believe me. He needs you to be his daughter. Just because he isn't prepared to have you live with him doesn't mean he doesn't need you and love you."

She kept on holding Katie's hand, gently stroking it with

her thumb. Her kindness freed the pain that Katie had held inside all winter. Claire handed her a tissue.

"Don't be embarrassed."

Grateful for the privacy of the corner booth, Katie dabbed at the tears. She hadn't realized how disappointed she was that Ed had no room for her. "It's just—" she finally stammered, "Mom's all settled with Steve. When the baby comes, they'll have their own family. Dad likes living alone. I don't fit anywhere. I'm a leftover from the divorce, something from the past."

Claire kept stroking Katie's hand. "No, not a leftover. You're the only thing that lasted from their marriage, but you're wrong when you say you belong to the past. You're a part of Ed's life right now. He loved showing you the city this week. He's excited that you're old enough to really do things with him. He's even thinking of asking you to come along on his next trip. Oh, damn!" Claire clamped her palm over her mouth. "I wasn't supposed to tell you that! He wanted to surprise you." She pursed her mouth in a sheepish grin. "Don't ever tell me a secret. I'm impossible. Oh, well. Anyway, he's so proud of you, of the way you're growing up. There are other ways to be part of someone's life besides living with them, you know. When someone cares about you, you're part of their life."

Katie listened quietly, her tears finished. She felt calmer.

"Let's get going. I want to show you the tiniest park in the city," Claire said.

Following Claire out to the street, Katie blinked and rubbed her eyes. Almost instantly, the sun and wind lifted her spirits. Storing the conversation away to think over later, she headed toward the park, trying to keep up with Claire.

Grandma's House

The next morning, on the train, Katie watched the city give way to towns and the towns turn to stretches of open fields. She didn't mind that Ed wasn't coming. She was tired from the city's pace and noise, from the intensity of being with her father and going, going all the time. Alone on the train, she relaxed.

The conductor called "Sea Gate," and, looking out the window, Katie saw the shops' striped awnings and window boxes, the harbor's skinny forest of masts, and the white bandstand with geraniums blooming around it. This was one place where she wouldn't have to wonder what to say or what to do.

Walking along the station platform, Katie spied her

grandmother's faded red Buick. Grandma gave her a hug that felt as firm as ever.

"I'm so glad to see you," Grandma said. "My errant son is off again, is he? To tell the truth, I'm glad. I was hoping for a chance to catch up with you."

"How do you feel, Grandma?"

"Fine. Just fine. They always dramatize these things." Grandma talked as she drove. Katie looked out the window. The town hadn't changed much in all the years she'd been coming. "Water's too cold, and it's too far from the city, thank goodness. Otherwise there'd be condominiums and hotels and who knows what other horrors. I hope I don't see it change in my lifetime," Grandma said. "I sound like an old crab, don't I?"

Katie hoped she'd never see it change, either. To her, the town was perfect. One movie house, a bookstore, a place to buy ice cream, and a little library that was open three days a week.

The car pulled into the driveway of the dark-shingled house, next to a blue VW.

"Eleanor's staying with me now—doctor's orders. I fussed at first, but I don't mind, really. We're used to each other. Thank God she doesn't chatter."

Eleanor, a widow who lived in the town, had been Grandma's housekeeper for years.

"She gave up her cottage, and we turned the upstairs wing into an apartment. She didn't want to leave her furniture. We get so attached to our things, you know? It was nice of her to be willing to move, don't you think?"

In the kitchen, Eleanor gave Katie a floury hug. "Oh, now, look what I've done. Gotten you covered with this.

Making a blueberry pie for dessert. We picked the berries this morning, your gran and I did."

She looked Katie carefully up and down. "You've shot up. Filled out, too. In the right places, if you know what I mean," she teased. "There's cookies in the tin. Oatmeal raisin. And iced tea in the fridge."

"I'll pour us each a glass," Grandma said. "You freshen up and meet me on the porch."

Katie went up to her room. She'd slept there every summer, in the blue room with the gables that faced the water. She loved to sit curled up on the window seat, looking out through the trees to the ocean. She could hear the waves at night when the sounds of the house had quieted.

She put her suitcase on the bed, changed into shorts and sneakers, and went to wash her face. Even the bathroom hadn't changed. The white wooden walls gleamed, and someone—maybe Grandma, maybe Eleanor—had placed a vase of zinnias next to the old-fashioned sink. There was a deep, claw-footed tub, and the mirror over the sink was framed with carved wooden flowers, each painted a different color. Katie studied her face for a moment. Had she changed? She'd felt so different at Ed's. But here she felt like her old self, before graduation, even before her mother's wedding. She felt light, free of worries. She dried her hands and bounded down the stairs, two at a time.

The next morning, Katie woke up slowly and stretched her body out, full-length, from her toes to her fingertips, uncurling like a new leaf. She'd taken a long bath before going to bed, soaking away the sticky city grit that seemed to have sifted in under her skin. The best thing about the old tub was its depth. You could lie with your head leaning back against the cool porcelain, and the water would cover you up to your chin.

Katie lay in bed enjoying the breeze that blew in the window. Filtered by the trees outside, the light shone alternately gold and green.

It was a curious thing, the serenity of Grandma's house. It wasn't just that Grandma was old. Ruth's grandmother was old, but fussy. She had to have her food prepared just so: no skin on the chicken; every scrap of fat removed from meat; milk served at room temperature; fruit cold from the refrigerator. She had so many rules: don't sing at the table; girls never whistle; chewing gum in public is coarse.

Ruth's grandmother made cutting remarks the way other people comment on the weather. Ruth was often the target. The other Ives girls were old enough to know how to avoid it. For some mysterious reason, the boys were excused altogether. Poor Ruth.

"Push your hair out of your eyes, dear. You look like a sheepdog." "Are you drinking enough water? Your skin looks terrible." "Must you wear those hideous sneakers? Sandals would look so much nicer." "Don't tell me you're still biting your nails, not at your age."

Katie had been with Ruth during some of these attacks, and had cringed for her. Ruth shrugged it off. "I just let it roll off my back. Mom says Granny's frustrated. When she was young, she had servants and cooks and stuff. She just can't get used to the change."

But Katie's grandmother was nothing like Ruth's. "Mellow Mother," Ed called her. Just as age had made Ruth's grandmother more critical, it had made Katie's grandmother more open-minded. She moved with a calm, graceful ease.

"At my age, dear, there's no longer any challenge in trying to beat the clock," she said. "I've won my race with time, or maybe time's won the race. Or maybe there never was a contest, just the two of us moving along together, arm in arm."

Katie loved that image. In her mind, she saw her grandmother strolling along the beach with a tall, thin man in a white suit and panama hat. His face was old, weathered by the sun. He had a wry smile and walked with a slight rolling swagger.

Grandmother's house was like her—easygoing, unhurried, in step and yet out of time. Things seemed ageless; some were faded, but nothing was worn out or broken.

Katie heard dishes rattling downstairs and Eleanor singing. The smell of bacon teased her stomach. She kicked off the sheet, jumped out of bed, pulled on jeans and a T-shirt, washed her face with cold water, and went down to breakfast in bare feet.

Grandma was reading the paper. "Sleep well?" she asked.

Katie nodded, and thanked Eleanor, who had just set a plate of eggs and bacon in front of her.

"What will you do today?" Grandma asked.

"Walk on the beach. Swim. Go to Rick's for a soda."

"You are like clockwork, child," Grandma chuckled. "Same routines every year. And they say older people are set in their ways."

After breakfast, they put on bathing suits and shorts and took a long walk down to the Point. Katie wore the old straw hat she'd found in the secondhand store. Grandma wore the same floppy white hat she'd worn for years. When she was hot, she dipped the hat in the ocean and put it on, dripping wet. The water ran down through her curls. She didn't care if it looked foolish. "Comfort first," she said.

They walked along the water's edge, letting the waves catch and cover their feet and ankles in sharp, cold water. At the Point, they climbed out to the farthest rock and sat on a ledge, legs dangling over the side. Below, waves rolled in, and sent occasional sprays up at them. Way out to sea, a sailboat slowly crossed the horizon. Nearer to shore, a few fishing boats started and stopped, started and stopped, checking lobster pots.

"I can't get over how much you've grown," Grandma said. "But there are years like that—big spurts. You can see it when you look at the rings of a tree. Some years are narrow, stingy, hardly any growth at all. Others are big, wide jumps. Sometimes growing years are hard, you know?" Her comment was also a question.

Katie stared down at the waves, hesitating for a moment. It was hard to decide how much to tell.

"Everything's different now."

"Of course."

"I didn't expect it to change."

"There's no way you would have known. What's different?"

"Everything. The house. Mom. It's strange. All of a sudden, everything I do is wrong, or at least a lot of it. I get on Steve's nerves. Or I used to. He complained about me all the time. Now he's stopped pretty much. Now I get on Mom's nerves instead."

"How's she feeling?"

"She looks like a blimp."

"Katie!"

"Really. She does. She wears this tent bathing suit and her legs stick out below like toothpicks. Her stomach bulges. It's disgusting."

"How do you expect her to look? She's pregnant."

"I know she's pregnant. Everyone knows that. It's no secret, I can tell you!"

"She's only six months along, isn't she?"

"I guess so. But she's huge, Grandma. A whale. A hippo."

Grandma couldn't help laughing. "All pregnant women look like that. How do you expect her to look?"

"She embarrasses me. She looks ridiculous."

"Why should that embarrass you?"

Katie stared at the horizon. She couldn't tell Grandma how she felt. It wasn't her mother being pregnant that made her twinge. But to get pregnant, she had to have sex, right? She felt creepy when she thought about it, her mother and Steve having sex, making love. Whatever words she used, the idea still made her squirm. She kicked her heels hard against the rock.

"Why should it embarrass you?" her grandmother repeated.

"She's too old to have a baby."

Grandma snorted. "Older women have babies every day, especially now."

"Nobody else in my class had a pregnant mother."

"That's why you're embarrassed?"

Katie shrugged and banged her heels some more. "That's part of it."

Grandma didn't press any further.

They sat together quietly for a few minutes, staring out at the water. A soft breeze roughened the surface. Katie let her eyes follow the zigzag of the wind as it turned the water a darker blue.

After a few minutes, Grandma said, "Let's have a swim and start back."

Katie followed her down the rocks, landing with a jump in the wet sand. They piled their clothes above the tide line and waded in. The veins in Grandma's legs showed through the pale skin like shadows of tree branches on snow, but her arms were freckled and brown. She walked regally into the waves, letting them smack her body. Katie ran in, hurtling through the water, and dived beneath a wave that was just beginning to crest. Once wet, they stayed shoulder-deep and jumped the waves together, gliding up and over the tops, letting the water support them. It felt so good, they stayed in until lunch.

After lunch, Grandma excused herself and went to nap. She'd never done it in past summers.

"She was really sick, wasn't she?" Katie asked Eleanor as they cleared away the dishes from lunch.

"Certainly was. Took her by surprise. She thought it was a cold, but turned out to be pneumonia. Then her heart acted up." Eleanor scraped the plates into the disposal. "One thing seemed to lead to another. It was an awful spell."

"Dad told me she wasn't feeling well in the spring, but I thought it was flu or something."

"He didn't want to worry you, I'm sure. And it was all done pretty quickly, the hospital part. The long part came after. Your gran just hated having to stay in bed. Complained all the time. You'd think she'd be too weak to argue, but not that one. Wanted to get up and work in the garden." Eleanor chuckled, shaking her head. "Finally the doctor came and spoke to her firmly. Then she settled down and stopped fussing. We could go for a walk every day. Even that was a lot, at first. You wouldn't know it to see her now, though, would you?"

Katie shook her head. Why hadn't she been told about this when it was going on? Her father had just said that Grandma was a little sick, but it was much more than that. What if Grandma had died? She would have found out when it was too late.

She finished drying the dishes and went out to the porch to read for a while.

Talking to Maddie

At the end of the first week at Grandma's Katie called
Maddie to see how long she could stay. She'd fallen into a
comfortable routine. Every day she spent the morning with
Gran at the beach, walking and swimming. They talked
about things, and around things. Then, after lunch, Katie
had the afternoons to herself while Gran napped. Sometimes she'd walk downtown and buy a soda or an ice-
cream cone. On Wednesdays and Fridays she stopped at
the library to poke around. Some days she went to pick
blueberries or rode the old three-speed bike that stood in
the garage. Some days she read on the porch.

 She wasn't lonely. It felt good to spend time alone,
knowing she'd be welcome back at the house whenever she
arrived. She didn't do a lot of thinking—just let her

thoughts come and go, not paying much attention to them. She wanted to stay longer, as long as she could. Maybe even until school started. Three more weeks.

"But Katie, we miss you here," Maddie said on the phone. Her voice sounded far away.

Katie didn't know what to say. She didn't care, and besides, she didn't believe it.

"You've been there a week already. Isn't that enough?"

"Grandma likes having me here."

"I'm sure she does. We like having you home, too. And Ruth misses you."

Katie was silent again.

Maddie filled in the pause. "You won't believe the garden. The tomatoes are getting ripe, and there's a melon that seems to double in size every few days."

"Mom, I like it here. I'm not in the way. I help out a lot. You can ask Grandma. I have all year to be home, but I only have the summertime for this." She was just repeating herself, she knew, but she didn't have anything else to add to her argument.

As she waited for an answer, she compared the two places in her mind. The beach at Grandma's was a stretch of sand, rocks, and cliffs; the pool at home was crowded and square, with that harsh chlorine smell. Who wouldn't want to stay here?

"I won't fight you, Katie. It's ridiculous to order you home. But I'll say it again, so you'll believe me. Steve and I miss you, and we wish you were here. We thought we'd take some day trips together, to the beach or maybe out to Lake Montclaire."

"You can still do those without me."

"The point is, we wanted to do them with you."

Katie was silent again.

Maddie waited for an answer. In the silence, Katie could hear faint shreds of other conversations over the wires. Finally Maddie spoke.

"Okay. You can stay for two more weeks. I want you home the week before school starts. Let me speak to Grandma."

Katie skipped in to get her grandmother. "I can stay! But she wants to talk to you now."

Grandma went to the phone. Katie followed at her heels, doing a little dance of excitement.

"Hello, Maddie. . . . I'm delighted to have her. . . . I know what you mean, sometimes you can't push them. . . . I'm sure it's been difficult. . . . I'm much better, dear. The doctor's convinced me to be cautious, but I'm feeling like my old self. And it's a comfort to have Katie with me when I swim. . . .

"You're right, of course. But I've always been a stubborn old crow, as you know. . . . Everyone makes me promise, but it's not in my nature to take it easy. . . .

"She's a good girl, Maddie. It's just a difficult time for the two of you. It often is between mothers and daughters, anyway, but with the marriage and the baby, it's intensified. . . .

"I'm sure. My sense is, it's been hard on everyone. I'm glad you've decided to let her stay. Sometimes it's good to be apart for a while. . . .

"Give my best to Steve, and be easy on yourself. All things in time. . . . I'll tell her. Good-bye, dear."

Grandma hung up the phone and put her arm around Katie's shoulders.

"You're mine for two more weeks. Your mother asked me to tell you again that she misses you. I believe her, Katie. I hope you do, too."

They walked out to the porch and sat together in the twilight, rocking. Two more weeks, Katie thought. Time stretched out here. She leaned her head against the back of the rocker and looked at the water. Even in the dusk she could see the line between the water and the sky. The water was darker, an opaque black, while the sky was a luminous gray. Later, at night, stars would clutter the sky, and if she sat and waited patiently, she might see shooting stars. They were hard to catch. Somehow, whenever you were looking at one place in the sky, a star zipped by in another, and you saw its motion only in the corner of your eye.

"Is it the right time for shooting stars?"

"Yes, they begin toward the middle of August. I've never understood why. Maybe we pass close by some other planet. Are you staying up?"

"Maybe sometime this week."

"Pick a clear night. There's a cloud bank rising tonight. Mid-week may be better. I'd join you, but the doctor would have my neck if he ever heard."

They rocked a little while longer.

"Well, I'm off to bed. Don't stay up too late," Grandma said.

Katie kissed her goodnight. For a while longer, she stayed out on the porch, rocking. Her mind kept drifting back to the conversation she'd had with Maddie. An uneasy feeling hung on.

Tomorrow maybe I'll write her a letter, she thought.

The Meeting

The letter waited until after lunch. Katie looked for some paper in the study and in the drawer of her night table, but found only index cards and a yellowed three-by-five pad. Determined to get the letter written, she headed downtown on the old bike.

The card store across from Rick's was long and narrow, with a single aisle down the middle. In the front, birthday and get-well cards filled the bins; in the back was a section of blank cards with photographs she'd seen before: a couple walking on a beach at sunset, a field of daisies, a basket of kittens. Why do they keep using the same old pictures when there are so many others to pick from, she wondered, remembering the cards she'd seen with Ed. She finally bought a small box of plain white stationery and went across the street to Rick's. She settled at a corner table with a root-beer float.

"Dear Mom . . ."

Well, that was a start, right? Now what?

"Thanks for letting me stay here at Grandma's. I'm having a good time."

Not a very exciting opening. She already knows that.

"I had fun at Dad's. We ate at lots of different restaurants—Japanese, Italian, Chinese, Greek. I heard a jazz group and went to the ballet. It was pretty modern. Not at all what I expected."

Should I tell her about Claire? Better not.

"We went to lots of museums and a play about an old woman trying to keep her family land. It was okay but a little long. I liked the jazz best."

How can I tell her about the clothes without mentioning Claire? Maybe she won't mind. She's got Steve, right?

"I went shopping in some antique clothes stores and found some neat things. It was fun."

Too boring. I'll start again. Good thing there's twenty sheets of paper in the box.

"Dear Mom, Thanks for letting me stay. I feel really good here. Not that I don't at home, but it's different here. I walk on the beach a lot, and swim. I'm sorry if I hurt your feelings this summer. I should have apologized after our fight. Maybe we can talk when I get home. I had a great time in the city. Dad and I ate out a lot. We saw a play, and went to museums and heard some great jazz. One of Dad's friends took me to see a dance company and we went shopping in secondhand clothing shops. Wait until you see what I got. Say hi to Steve for me. Love, Katie."

She took a sip of her float. The ice cream had melted, and a puddle rimmed the bottom of the glass.

As she folded the letter and put it in an envelope, she noticed a boy sitting at the next table writing postcards. He must have come in while she was working on the letter. He looked up and grinned.

"Writing home," he explained, nodding at the postcard.

"Me, too."

"Who are you visiting?"

"My grandmother."

"No kidding! Me, too. Do you come here a lot?"

"Every summer."

"This is my first time. My grandparents moved here last winter when my grandfather retired. My name is Paul. Paul Blackwell."

"I'm Katie Henderson."

"Look, I don't usually talk to people. I mean, I don't want you to think that I always talk to strangers in places like this. But I don't know anybody here. Do you play tennis? I mean, would you like to play tennis with me? I saw some courts behind the fire station. We could sign up."

He finally stopped. Katie grinned. This kid was even more awkward than she was. He grinned back.

"I'd love to play tennis. Let's see what times are open."

They walked over to the fire station and signed up for three the next afternoon.

"See you tomorrow," Katie said.

"Okay. Meet you here." He walked off with his hands in his pockets, whistling. At the corner, he looked back and waved.

I'm not a very good tennis player, Katie thought, but it

was too late to worry about that now. On the way home, she tried to remember what he looked like. Tall. Hair somewhere between blond and brown. Thin face with dark eyebrows. Eyes blue? She hadn't noticed. Not too handsome, not ugly. Kind of ordinary. Like me, she thought.

Serious players avoided the courts behind the firehouse. Large cracks scarred both sides and the nets sagged in the middle. A slight breeze tried unsuccessfully to counteract the sun's heat. Katie's forehead was dripping by the end of the first rally.

Paul hit the ball with a clean, even stroke. He didn't try for spin or aim at the corners, but his shots were strong and fast. Watching him step into his stroke and swing through, Katie was struck by the mix of grace and power. Yesterday's awkwardness was replaced by confidence.

Katie's own tennis was haphazard. She'd learned to play in a summer program when she was nine, lined up with a lot of other neighborhood kids, batting balls against a wooden backstop three mornings a week. As she got older, she'd practiced with Ruth down at the high-school courts but often quit in embarrassment when their wild shots repeatedly interrupted a serious game on the next court.

Playing with Paul, Katie discovered that your game improves when your partner is good. She watched his strokes, tried hard to copy the way he moved, and, to her amazement, hit the ball squarely over the net more often than not.

"Nice," he would call.

"Good stroke."

"Step into it."

"Keep your racket even and swing right into the ball. Don't be afraid to wallop it. Good!"

When the face of her racket was even, the balls didn't fly wildly up in the air. Her shots got longer and stayed lower than the soft, high pats she used to hit.

"I like slamming it," she told Paul during a break. "You're probably used to playing with really good people."

"I'm having fun. Want to play again tomorrow?"

Katie nodded.

They played again for an hour on Wednesday. Then Thursday was exceptionally hot. After half an hour, Paul asked, "Want to quit?"

"How about another fifteen minutes, and then we'll go for a swim."

"I didn't bring my suit."

"Neither did I. We can ride home, change and meet at the Point."

Katie got there first and climbed out to the edge. She spotted Paul at a distance. He loped down the beach, his towel around his neck. Seeing her up on the rocks, he grinned and waved both arms over his head, not caring if he looked foolish in his exuberance.

He likes me, she thought. She hunched her shoulders and hugged her knees. This wasn't the first time someone had liked her. On and off through grade school she'd been the object of short crushes.

In kindergarten, a boy named Tim gave her caramels every day for a week. In third grade, she sat beside a boy named Curtis with very blue eyes ringed with thick dark lashes. She loved him from October on, but it wasn't until midwinter that he reciprocated and kissed her by the water fountain.

In sixth grade, all the boys liked Tanya Holmes, the first girl in the class to really need a bra. Some boys bumped into her on purpose, trying to feel her breasts with the sides of their arms.

In seventh grade, Katie heard that Robbie Cronin liked her. His friend Greg told Paula, who lived next door to him, and Paula told Ruth, and Ruth, of course, told Katie. She waited a week for Robbie to call her up because Ruth had said he said he was going to. But he never did. So she never knew if he really liked her or not.

Paul found footholds up the rocks and walked out to the ledge, where she was sitting. He eased himself down beside her, close enough for his warm arm to brush against hers.

"You look nice with the wind blowing your hair like that," he said.

A little self-conscious, she reached to smooth it down.

"I've never been up here before." When he smiled, he had two tiny dimples.

They watched the waves move in toward the shore.

"Ready to swim?" he asked.

She nodded. He pulled her up and kept hold of her hand as they climbed down to the beach.

"I've got to get in fast," he said.

They ran in together, high-stepping over the surf and belly-flopping into a wave that had started to crash. They surfaced in the lull on the other side. Paul flung his head to the side, shaking his hair out of his eyes. Katie pushed hers back and floated easily on the swells.

As if the idea had occurred to him at that very second, Paul suddenly pulled her toward him and kissed her. It felt so good and comfortable that she didn't feel startled, just a little out of breath.

He didn't kiss her again that afternoon, but they held hands all the way up the beach to their bikes.

Spending Time with Paul

Katie saw Paul every day during the two weeks she had left. On sunny afternoons they played tennis and swam. When it rained, they played Scrabble on Grandma's porch, where the smell of pine and salt water drifted through the screens.

They talked so easily. And joked. And teased. And kissed. Knowing that Paul liked her made Katie feel warm all over. Even when she wasn't with him, she was more sure of herself. His attention gave her confidence. Sometimes she imagined telling Ruth about him. She'll be surprised, Katie thought.

Katie still walked and swam every morning with her grandmother. In the middle of her last week, the morning tide was extra low, perfect for picking mussels. Grandma knew a cove with tidal pools and rocks thick with seaweed below the tide line. The mussels clumped together, making it easy to collect a bucketful. After the sand and mud had been scrubbed off, Grandma steamed the mussels in garlic, wine, and herbs. She invited Paul to join them for lunch. They ate outside in the back garden on a white metal table covered for the occasion with a blue-and-white woven cloth.

"Go and pick a bouquet," Grandma told Katie. "There are plenty of flowers in the field behind the hedge."

Katie picked a bunch and put them in the big white pitcher that Grandma gave her. They filled the center of the table in a burst of color.

Paul arrived, looking scrubbed. His hair, damp from a shower, was slicked flat on his head, but his cowlick had already started to spring free. Instead of jeans, he wore pressed khaki pants and a light-blue shirt. After a few moments of nervousness, when his foot jiggled and he pressed his hair smooth again and again, he relaxed.

They ate the mussels dipped in butter with crusty French bread that Eleanor had baked in long, thin pans. Grandma and Eleanor drank white wine. Katie and Paul drank French cider, halfway between apple juice and wine. It made Katie lightheaded.

After lunch, Grandma took her nap and Katie and Paul rode out to Heron Beach. They locked their bikes to a sapling and walked in through the woods. Moss hung in clumps and wild grape and ivy vines smothered the trees.

"Spooky," Paul whispered.

"It feels as if no one has been here for a long time. Like

time stopped," Katie said softly. She was almost tiptoeing, unconsciously trying not to break the spell.

The forest ended at the edge of a white-sand cove, littered only with broken lines of seaweed and a few old logs. Katie spread her towel next to a big piece of driftwood and lay down on her back with the log as a headrest. Paul stretched out alongside her. They lay with their eyes closed, enjoying the sun and the silence. Tiny waves rippled on the shore in a soothing rhythm.

Paul rolled over onto his side and propped his head on his hand. Katie knew he was studying her. Very lightly, he began to trace his finger up and down her arm, then along her profile.

"Tickles," she said, smiling.

"Why do you have to go?" It was the first time either of them had mentioned it. "Maybe Sunday won't come."

"Right. Time will stand still. We'll stay here in the forest like Sleeping Beauty."

"But she was all alone. The Prince wasn't with her. You're luckier. I'm already here."

"Ha! Modest, aren't you? Anyway, everyone will miss us."

"They won't even know we're gone. Time will stand still, remember?"

Katie closed her eyes again and lay holding Paul's hand. What would it be like to stand still in time? What would she miss? Bad things or good? It felt so nice to lie close beside Paul. She wanted to stay and have it be August forever. But she also felt a tug of excitement at the idea of fall and its beginnings. High school, new kids, new courses and teachers. Even the new baby.

"I bet it's late," she said after a while. "We better get back." She stood up and surveyed the cove. The sun had dropped behind the trees. Shadows sprawled across the sand. Paul let her pull him to his feet. He followed her out to the bikes.

Three more days, she thought as she pedaled back to Grandma's. If I try, maybe I can remember everything that happens.

But the days went by quickly, smooth as water in a wide river with a fast current. She couldn't step onto the shore to get a better look. She could only let herself be pulled along.

The Dance

On Saturday, her last night before going home, Katie went with Paul to the August Moon Dance at the Boat Club.

"My grandparents want to introduce me to all their pals. It's their version of Show and Tell. Everyone will check to see how neatly I've combed my hair," Paul said.

"It's a hopeless case," Katie said, eyeing his cowlick.

Paul nodded. "Not only that, but the kids are snobs. They check you out to see if you're the right type. 'What school do you go to?' I say, 'P.S. 173, Junior High School 109, Smithville Regional High School.' That shuts them up. They're so busy saying Exeter or Saint Paul's that they interrupt each other just to get it in."

"I thought you went to prep school, too."

"Yeah, but I'm not going to tell those turkeys. They just

want to peg you. Figure out if you're worth talking to. They're a bunch of jerks, I'm telling you."

Paul pushed the sand angrily with the edge of his tennis racket.

"It means a lot to my grandparents. So what the hell, it won't kill me. Come with me? After they get through showing me off, we can go down on the dock and dance by ourselves, or just listen to the music."

"Sounds nice. I'll ask Grandma."

"Of course you may go," Grandma told Katie. "But I want you all to myself Sunday morning. We'll have a garden breakfast together before your train."

Saturday night, before the dance, Paul's grandparents took them to dinner at a waterfront restaurant. His grandfather showed Katie his technique for eating lobster.

"First you break off the claws, then you crack the body this way. The tail is the sweetest part."

He acted as if he were initiating her into an elite society, the kind with a password and a special handshake. The plastic bib with the red lobster printed on it was the insignia.

"Squeeze some lemon into the butter, then dip in the lobster meat."

He demonstrated enthusiastically, dripping butter generously down the front of his bib.

Katie managed to keep the butter off her dress, the green one she'd worn to the graduation dance.

When they reached the club, Paul's grandparents introduced them to several gray-haired couples sitting in the lounge. It was just like playing a part, all dressed up and acting polite. She smiled, shook hands, and said "How do you do?" over and over again. Several people knew her grandmother, even though she wasn't a member. She heard comments behind her: "What a sweet girl." "Don't they look cute?"

Finally, with a nod from Paul's grandfather and a kiss from his grandmother, they were free.

They wandered down toward the music. By the boathouse, kids clustered in groups, laughing and talking. If she'd been alone, Katie would have shriveled inside, imagining what they were saying about her. But with Paul beside her, his arm draped comfortably over her shoulders, she passed by nonchalantly, letting their glances roll off.

"Let's dance on the dock," Paul said, leading her down the sloping gangplank to the empty float.

Music drifted down from the boathouse and mixed with the soft slap of water against the pilings. Paul guided her carefully, staying in the center, away from the edge. They took little steps, hardly moving at all. His cheek felt cool and smooth against her forehead. His shirt smelled freshly ironed. Resting her head on his shoulder, she watched the reflection of the colored lights hanging from the eaves of the boathouse.

During the fast songs, they sat on the edge of the dock holding hands and swinging their feet over the water. About ten-thirty, the moon rose, deep yellow at first, then fading as it climbed.

"I just wish you could stay," Paul said, breaking the long silence. He squeezed her hand.

Katie nodded. She had no words. Being close to someone was new to her. What did you say when you had to leave? What was she supposed to feel?

"Will you write to me this year when I'm at school? I never get mail," Paul said.

"Sure. I like to write letters."

"I don't, but I like to get them. That makes it even, right?"

They sat in silence some more, leaning slightly against each other.

"We better get back soon. My grandparents may be looking for us," Paul said.

But instead of standing up, he kissed her for a long time.

Back at the boathouse, the music was loud and fast. They joined the crowd, but even when they were dancing fast, Paul held her hand.

Katie watched him dance. His hair flopped as he bobbed from side to side. He shuffled and bounced to the drumbeat. Some boys danced with rubber bodies, twisting shoulders and legs, rippling their spines like snakes. Paul was just the sweat-and-bounce type, very ordinary.

Close to midnight, the older people came and stood along the walls of the boathouse, watching. Paul's grandparents smiled and pointed out Paul and Katie to their friends. It was embarrassing to dance with an audience. Soon, Paul's grandfather caught their eye and tapped his watch.

"Pumpkin time," Paul said.

At the end of the song, they left the floor.

"Have fun?" his grandmother asked.

His grandfather handed Paul a handkerchief to mop off his face.

On the ride home, Paul sat close to Katie in the back seat. When they reached her house, she said goodnight and thanked his grandparents.

106:

"Don't wait for me," Paul said to them. "I'll walk home from here."

"Paul, dear, it's late," his grandmother started to protest, but his grandfather winked and said, "Fine. We'll see you there. Good night, Katie." He drove off, with his wife still spluttering.

"He's a good guy," Paul said, linking his arm with Katie's. "Take a walk?"

She nodded, happy to have some more time with him. The upstairs lights were off in the house. Grandma and Eleanor would have gone to bed by eleven or even earlier. They'd said the back door would be open. Katie was proud to be trusted.

"Just a short walk. I told Grandma I'd be home about one."

They headed out toward the water. Trees and hedges threw long shadows in the moonlight. A breeze came up as they neared the cliffs. Noticing Katie shiver, Paul draped his jacket around her shoulders, anchoring it with his arm.

They walked until they reached the rocks, then sat looking up at the sky. The moon had disappeared. Katie spotted a shooting star out of the corner of her eye. Then a long streak of light gleamed across the center of the sky.

"Fireworks," Paul said. "Good luck."

"I thought it meant that someone was dying."

He shrugged. "This is my lucky summer. Everything's lucky—black cats, ladders, everything."

"Why?"

"I met you, that's why. You're my good-luck charm."

She jabbed him in the ribs. The conversation stopped as they kissed again.

"What would it feel like if we kissed all night?" Paul

wondered as they paused for breath.

"Maybe our lips would get numb from lack of circulation," Katie said. "They'd just fall off."

Paul eyed her sideways with a frown. "Very romantic."

"You're the one who brought it up," she answered, laughing. "We'd better stop, anyway. I've got to get home."

"Me, too, before Gran sends out the cruiser."

They walked back slowly, Katie's shoes wet with dew and squeaking slightly. Her dress felt damp, too. She yawned.

"Good night," she said when they reached the back porch. "I'll write."

"I'll call you this week," Paul said. "I'm going to miss you."

She nodded.

After a last kiss, she went inside. Upstairs, she got ready for bed, toweling off her feet to warm and dry them. Slipping under the covers, she snuggled into the smooth sheets and pulled the blanket up around her shoulders.

Neither of us said "I love you," she thought. That would be too much. Why don't people ever say "I like you"? It sounded funny. Why? she wondered, then let the thought go, too tired to pursue it.

Going Home

Katie dozed on the train, her head resting against the window. She woke up at Munroe, one stop before home. Groggy from the nap, she rubbed her eyes and started to collect her things. The big suitcase was in the overhead rack. She slid it down and left it beside her seat. She fit her magazines and the mystery Paul had lent her into her shoulder bag. Then she watched for the familiar landmarks.

She felt rumpled and sticky. After a long breakfast with Grandma, all she'd done was sit all day, trying to read, but daydreaming instead. Trains used to excite her, but she felt much older now, older than before she'd left for Ed's. How would it feel to be back? She'd go over to Ruth's and tell her all about it. Tell about Paul. But she hadn't written. She'd promised, but forgotten. The last thing she sent was the postcard she'd bought with Claire, an old photo of women in bathing dresses. The whole time at Grandma's she'd never thought of Ruth. It had only been three weeks. It seemed much longer.

The train pulled in, and Katie struggled down the steps with her bags and waited on the edge of the empty platform. Across the street, two old men sat on a bench in the park, watching the occasional car go by. The swings were empty. The flag hung limp in the hot air. The gravel in the parking lot radiated heat. Funny, she'd never noticed how small the town was. When she first started school, the walk down Main Street took forever.

Her mother's car turned the corner and drove up the street into the lot. Katie waved.

"Hi, sweetheart," Maddie said, opening the door and climbing out. "You look WONDERFUL!" She gave Katie a big hug and kissed her on the cheek. "I missed you. Really I did!"

"I missed you, too."

"Ruth's been calling and calling. She keeps asking, 'When's she getting home?'"

They loaded the suitcase and bag into the back seat. Maddie eased in behind the wheel. "If I get much bigger, I don't know how I'll fit. I can move the seat back to make room for my belly, but my arms aren't that long."

She'd gotten a lot bigger in the past month. How much bigger would she get? Katie wondered.

"The doctor thinks we might have counted wrong. The baby might come in late October.

"Are you sure?" Katie asked.

"No. Not sure at all. Could still be November. But it's easy to miss the start. It wasn't anything we planned. Everything's an approximation, anyway. Mother Nature's too sly for science to pin her down." Maddie smiled as she drove. She reached across the seat and patted Katie's hand. "I'm glad you're home."

Katie nodded but her mind was still on the news. October. The baby. She hadn't even thought about it. What would it look like?

"Where's it going to sleep?"

"The baby? In the study. I moved my desk out into the hall, and Steve painted the walls white with green trim. You'll like it. There's a border of ducks. It sounds silly, doesn't it? I guess I'm nesting."

Maddie took her upstairs to show her when they reached the house. Katie stood in the middle of the room. A white crib took up one corner, and a wicker changing table stood in front of the window. The only other piece of furniture was a rocker.

"Steve found the rocker at a yard sale," Maddie said. "The crib was yours, believe it or not. I gave it to Aunt Elizabeth for Jamie, and she hung on to it. I think it's great. Your old crib. Maybe it's an omen. I hope you two will be close, I really do."

Maddie's voice quivered. Katie looked over in surprise. Maddie's eyes glistened with tears.

"I'm glad you're home, sweetheart."

"I am, too."

After she'd changed, Steve took her out back to the garden. Instead of the thin young plants she remembered, rows of leafy vegetables stood green and sturdy. The tomato plants had stretched up and filled out their wire cages. Even the marigolds were bushy.

"Take a look at the zucchini. It's trying to take over the back corner," Steve said, laughing. "Back! Get back, you monster!" He waved his arms at it. "And I don't even like zucchini."

"Me, neither." Katie spotted one the size of her arm, nestled under the dark, spiky leaves. "What will we do with it all?"

"Make zucchini bread. Zucchini spaghetti sauce. Zucchini pizza. Zucchini ice cream?"

"We can always throw it out," Katie said.

"Good idea. Your mother will have a fit, but now that you're home, it's two to one against zucchini. Thank God you're back!"

Katie looked at him suspiciously but he seemed to really mean it.

Catching Up

Katie called Ruth after dinner.

"About time you got back!" Ruth said. "You wouldn't believe how boring it was here. Did you have fun? What was it like?"

Katie didn't know where to begin. How could she fit it all into a phone conversation? "It was great," she said lamely.

"What did you do?"

"In the city, we went to museums, saw a dance company, heard some jazz."

Ruth whistled. "Jazz? Since when do you like jazz? What happened to rock?"

Katie laughed. "I still like it, but jazz is different."

"What else did you do?"

"At Grandma's, I went swimming and played tennis every day. And I met this boy. . . ."

"A BOY! That's more like it! What's his name, what's he look like?"

Katie didn't want to go into detail while sitting in the upstairs hall. Maddie or Steve might walk by any minute.

"His name's Paul. I'll tell you about it tomorrow. What do you want to do?"

"Let's ride out to Fisher's Pond."

"That's far!"

"So? We'll leave early. We can find a good spot all to ourselves. Then you can fill me in on all the juicy details. Remember, this is Lorna Love-love you're talking to."

They left at nine and reached the pond at midmorning.

"Follow me, I know a place." Ruth pointed to the shore opposite the beach area.

She led Katie past the beach, already filling up with mothers in folding chairs and toddlers with pails and shovels.

The far side of the pond was shallow, with grassy banks. They spread their towels and stripped off their clothes, damp from the long ride. Katie waded out until she could dive, the clear, soft water gliding against her skin.

Ruth popped up beside her with a grin and a splash. Together they headed back toward the towels.

"Now tell me everything," Ruth said when they'd sprawled in the sun.

"Okay. First I got up every morning and ate breakfast," Katie teased. "Sometimes I had an egg, sometimes cereal, and once or twice I had pancakes."

"Very funny. I mean everything about Paul."

It sounded strange to hear Ruth say his name so casually. She said it as if she knew him, but she didn't know him at all. She could have said, Tell me about Jim, or Tell me about Louis. It would all have been the same to her. But to Katie, Paul was Paul, someone distinct, special.

She tried to describe him. "He's kind of tall. His hair is in between brown and blond, and it's very straight, except for this cowlick." Katie smiled, thinking of Paul trying to force down that stubborn spring of hair. "He's got in-between eyes, too. Green and brown, with speckles."

"Okay, enough description. He sounds cute. Get to the mushy part."

"What do you think this is, one of those teen romance books? 'First Love'? 'Steamy Summer'?"

"Right, tell it just the way it was," Ruth said.

Katie stalled. She didn't want to go into details, describing how they'd kissed or how she'd felt. It seemed disloyal, sharing things that had happened between Paul and herself. She hated to think of him telling his friends. Besides, if she tried to put it all into words, it might make it seem ordinary or even silly.

"It's hard to describe. We played tennis almost every day, and we swam. Sometimes I'd go over to his house, and sometimes he came over to Grandma's. We played Scrabble. Then, just before I left, we went to a dance at the Boat Club." She shrugged. "That's about it. He's really nice."

Ruth looked disgusted. "That has to be the deadest description I have ever heard. Did you kiss?"

Katie nodded.

"A lot?"

She nodded again, starting to blush.

"Is that all you did?"

"Ruth! Cut it out!"

"Ah, too shy to tell? Come on! I thought we were best friends! If I had anything to tell, I wouldn't hold out on *you*."

"You don't know. You might. It just isn't the kind of thing you tell about." Katie watched Ruth, trying to gauge her reaction. She didn't want to make her angry, especially on their first day together.

But Ruth looked confused and hurt, and even a little jealous, Katie realized with surprise. She'd always been sure that Ruth would be the first to have a boyfriend. But it had happened to her instead.

She tried again. "I'd tell you if I could, but it sounds weird. It wasn't so much. We spent a lot of time together, but it wasn't like on a date. We just hung around together."

Ruth looked relieved. "Oh, you mean like friends?"

"Sort of." Katie knew this wasn't completely honest. "But it was more than that. He was like a boyfriend and like a friend, too."

Ruth nodded, not fully satisfied.

Anxious to change the subject, Katie said, "What happened with the lifeguard?"

"That girl I saw him with at the movies started coming to the pool every day. She'd plop herself down at the foot of his chair and guard him. No way could I talk to him after that. Once or twice I tried, but she glared at me so hard that I forgot what I was going to say."

116:

"Bad luck," Katie said. "But there'll be tons of boys at the high school."

Ruth grinned. "Don't I know it? I'm ready. Boy, am I ever ready. HIGH SCHOOL, WATCH OUT! HERE I COME."

Her voice echoed out over the lake.

Katie tossed a handful of grass into the air like confetti.

Starting School

School started the next Tuesday.

"Did you get a letter from Paul yet?" Ruth asked as they walked toward the high school that morning.

"Not yet. It's only been a week."

"Did you write to him?"

"I tried, but it sounded jerky."

"What are you going to do?"

Katie shrugged. Maybe she'd try to write again in a few days. The time with Paul seemed as if it had happened to a different person.

Up ahead, she spotted a cluster of boys from eighth grade. They looked like midgets next to the older high-school boys. Do we look that small, too? she wondered.

After much discussion, Katie and Ruth had decided to wear skirts on the first day. It was hot for pants, shorts were too informal, and dresses would be babyish. "I don't want to look like a bigger version of a kindergarten kid all dressed up for school," she explained to Maddie at breakfast.

"You sound nervous. Are you?" Maddie asked.

"It's a big school. I don't know many kids. Just the ones from Green."

"You'll meet others quickly. Everyone's in the same boat."

Not really, Katie thought. She'd heard rumors of older kids hazing the ninth-graders. Initiations. Stairways to keep away from. Jocks hang out by the Annex. Punks have the back stairway. But Ruth's sisters said it wasn't true. Nothing ever happened to us, they said. But they were tall, protected by looks, with the right combination of earrings in each earlobe and thick, shiny hair that couldn't look bad. Katie had no such armor.

"I wish we had the same homeroom," she said to Ruth. "Mine's 210."

"Mine's 218."

Trying to stay together, they worked their way down the first-floor hall, weaving in and out of chattering clusters. How *are* you? You look *great.* Hey, baby, how's it going? Who's he with? How's she doing? What did you do? Down at the beach. Driver's Ed. Got my license. See you later. Quit shoving. Save me a seat.

The second-floor was less congested.

"Let's eat lunch together," Ruth said. "Meet you at the bottom of the stairs."

Katie had an urge to give Ruth a hug, the way you'd say good-bye to someone you might not see again. But she settled for a wave. "Good luck," she said as Ruth moved away, carried along by the momentum of the crowd.

"You, too," Ruth called back.

First there was homeroom: forms in triplicate, locker assignments, schedules. The room was hot to begin with, and the temperature rose steadily as the sun beat through the windows and glared off the polished linoleum.

"Enjoy it. It won't be this clean again all year," said Mr. Durant, the laconic homeroom teacher.

Announcements droned from the loudspeaker, the voices distorted and blurred with static. Older students came and went, delivering batches of forms, packages of pastel cards, and messages.

"Paper work, bane of society," said Mr. Durant. "Hang in there, everyone. Freshman assembly in fifteen minutes."

Katie watched a fly make frantic figure eights. It finally found the window and sailed out. To freedom, Katie thought, feeling bored already. She knew only one other person in the room, George Herrick. He'd been at Green School, too, but since he hadn't been in her section, she didn't know him well.

"No assigned seats, just answer loud and clear when I take attendance." Mr. Durant was low-key, relaxed, and confident. "And be on time. I hate to write up late slips." He propped his feet up on the drawer of his desk.

He thinks he's one of the gang, Katie thought. She distrusted his casualness, preferring to have the rules clearly stated and a certain strictness to go by.

When the bell rang for assembly, she followed the crowd

downstairs to the auditorium. She couldn't find Ruth but spotted Susan and Barb from Green, and sat with them.

"Anybody cute in your homeroom?" Barb asked her.

Katie hadn't even looked. Boys had been Barb's main focus since sixth grade. Even now, she was scanning the crowd as it moved down the aisles and into the seats, pointing out boys who caught her eye.

"What about that tall guy with the curly hair. I think he went to Brookside. The guy with the red hair is all right, too."

Katie paid no attention. She watched the stage instead. Upperclassmen took seats on either side of the microphone, looking cocky and nonchalant. They're the big shots, Katie thought. I bet they run all the clubs and activities. Yearbook, newspaper, student council. They acted as if they knew they were being watched. One girl with very short hair, like a little boy's summer crew cut, crossed her legs and tucked one foot behind her calf. The boy next to her patted her on the shoulder as if she'd said something funny. They look like they're playing parts in a play, Katie thought.

A man with glasses walked up to the microphone.

"Settle down, please. Everyone find a seat. Good. That's good." He paused until the room had quieted down. "I'm Mr. Maxwell, the principal. You'll be seeing a lot of me in the next four years here at Mayfield. Some of you may see more of me than others." He paused for laughter, which came only feebly from the audience. "I'm here to welcome you to Mayfield High School and to introduce some of the people you need to know, and some who can help you get involved here."

Katie's mind started to wander as the principal's voice rumbled on and on.

What's the point? Who cares who's in charge of the yearbook or when the cheerleading tryouts are. We'll never remember all these people, Katie thought. She was surprised by her own cynicism. Why aren't I more interested in all this? she wondered. I wish I were back at Grandma's, walking along the beach. She floated in a daydream, remembering Paul, until Barb and Susan stood up suddenly, jolting Katie back to the present with a start.

"What do we do now?" she asked.

"Didn't you hear him? We follow the schedule. Half an hour in each class. Get books, meet the teachers. That's it."

Katie looked at the clock. Four classes before lunch, three after. She scanned the crowd for Ruth but couldn't find her. She followed the crowd out and set off in search of Room 327. English with McCready.

The Eggsperiment

"English and Health are the best," Katie told Maddie at the end of the first week. "Earth Science is boring. I don't see why we have to take it."

Katie sat cross-legged on the grass, watching her mother. It was warm for September, almost as warm as summer, but the sun wasn't as strong and a light breeze stirred the heads of the chrysanthemums. Maddie was hanging out clothes on the backyard line. She pinned up underpants with floppy stretch panels in front, baggy enough for a hippo.

"Mom, remember George and Martha, the two hippos? Your underpants could be Martha's."

"That's mean!" Maddie chuckled, holding up a pair and looking them over. "Well, there's two of us fitting in them, remember." She pinned up a pair of gray maternity slacks. The waist was so wide that the legs looked ridiculously thin below.

"Humpty Dumpty pants," Katie joked. "That reminds me of this crazy project in Health. Wait, I'll read you the rules."

Katie pulled her binder out of her knapsack. Flipping through the sections, she found the page she was looking for.

"'In the Eggsperiment, you each will become the proud parent—mother or father—of a bouncing baby egg. Each baby will have two parents. Since this is the age of equal rights, the mother and father will be equally responsible for the care of the baby.'"

Katie looked up. Maddie had stopped hanging clothes and was listening with an amused expression.

"Want to hear the rest?" Maddie nodded, so Katie continued. "Here are the rules. '1. Parent teams will be picked by drawing names. You are not "married" for life—just for one week. 2. Babies will be given to you on Monday. They must be cared for until the next Monday. 3. Each parent team must keep a daily record of who is taking care of the baby. Account for each hour of the day. Babies cannot be left alone. They must be handled gently. 4. Babies usually eat every four hours or so. On your daily record, keep track of these feedings. Parents should share the feeding responsibility. 5. At the end of the week you will submit a complete record of the care-and-feeding schedule and return to me a healthy (unbroken!) egg baby. Grades will be determined based on the quality of care your baby has received.'"

124:

"Sounds wild," Maddie said. "Your baby'll arrive before this one." She patted her stomach. "You were bald as an egg when you were born. I bet this egg baby looks just like you."

"Ha! At least I don't wear Humpty Dumpty pants."

Katie lay back on the grass. Everything felt perfect. The first week of school had gone fast. Nothing terrible had happened. She'd gotten lost a few times but that was all. She'd even tried out for field hockey and made the freshman team. It was a lot like soccer. All in all, it wasn't a bad start.

"So who's your partner?" Maddie asked. "The egg's father?"

"Joel Hunneman."

"Did he go to Green?"

"No. Brookside. He lives out past the cemetery."

Maddie whistled and raised her eyebrows. The houses out there were huge. "Maybe you can get his maid to take care of the egg all week."

"Mom, that's stereotyping. He's nice."

"Rich people can be nice. I didn't say he wasn't nice."

"But that's what you meant."

"Okay. So I'm prejudiced against rich people. I admit it."

Katie let it drop.

"What will you name the egg—the baby, I mean. It's got to have a name. Think of all the possibilities. Humpty. Eggbert."

"What about Shelly?"

"Good yoke."

"Mom! That's terrible!"

"So's Shelly."

On Monday, Mrs. Ortiz gave out blank birth certificates to each of them. "List the names of both parents and then give your baby's name."

Katie and Joel filled out the form until they reached the line for the baby's name. Katie told Joel all the names she and Maddie had joked about.

"Too obvious. I want something subtle. Like Runyon," Joel said.

"Runyon? I never heard of it."

"Damon Runyon was a writer. Runyon, like runny. I hate runny eggs."

"Me, too. Let's not call it Runyon."

"Okay, but think of something less obvious than Shelly."

Katie turned the word "egg" over and over in her mind. Dreg was too negative. Peg wasn't bad. She thought some more. "How about Meg?"

"What if it's a boy?"

"We can call him Bert. Short for Eggbert."

Katie raised her hand. "Mrs. Ortiz, how do we know if it's a boy or a girl?"

"You come up and flip the coin."

It was a nickel with a pink circle on one side and a blue circle on the other. Joel flipped it, caught it, and slapped it on the back of his hand. It came up pink.

"Meg it is," he said.

Katie wrote "Meg Henderson-Hunneman" on the line.

When the documents were filled out, each team received an egg. Mrs. Ortiz wrote the name on the bottom with a laundry marker. Then she stamped it.

"This way I can be sure that the egg you give back is the one you started out with."

"Mrs. Ortiz, can I draw a face on mine?" asked a girl in the front row.

"Certainly. I suggest you use a felt-tip pen, preferably waterproof so it won't smudge."

"Mrs. O., how am I supposed to carry this? It's raw, right? What if it cracks? It'll mess up my books."

"That's the first of many problems you'll have to solve. These egg babies need special handling. They can't be left in lockers. They need air. They need soft, open containers that will protect them. They can't be left alone. If you want to go out, you either have to take them along or get an egg-sitter."

"This is ridiculous," said Joel.

"It's just for a week," Mrs. Ortiz said. "Then we'll draw some conclusions."

Mrs. Ortiz had a lot of little boxes and some scraps: there were containers that had held Chinese food, ice cream, and yogurt—all carefully washed—along with pieces of fabric, foam rubber, toweling, and sponges to line them.

"I suggest that you each make your own container, or should I say cradle."

"Cradle, cage, who cares? This is embarrassing," Joel whispered.

Katie could tell that he meant it. He struck her as a quiet, private person, not someone who enjoyed being silly. It was hard not to feel foolish doing this experiment.

Katie picked a Chinese food container, and Joel chose a small milk carton. They lined the insides of the "cradles" with foam.

"What happens if this egg breaks? I bet we fail," Joel said.

"Where is the egg?" Katie asked.

"In my pocket, nice and cozy, providing no one bumps into me. How are we going to divide the schedule?"

"Let's trade days. I'll start, then give you the egg tomorrow," Katie said.

The bell rang for the end of class.

"Good luck," Joel said. "Here's Meg. Take good care of her."

"Thanks," Katie said. She put her knapsack on, picked up the white container, and went out into the busy hall feeling sillier with every step she took. In Earth Science, she put the egg on her desk alongside her notebook. No one else in the class had been in Health.

"What's that?" asked the girl beside her.

"It's my egg baby," said Katie, wishing immediately she'd just said it was an egg. "It's a Health project," she added lamely.

The girl looked inside the container. Katie was glad she hadn't drawn a face on the egg.

"Cute," said the girl, rolling her eyes. "What's its name?"

"Meg," Katie said.

"Meg Egg. *Real* cute," the girl said sarcastically.

She means weird, Katie thought. She wanted to put the carton on the floor before anyone else noticed it, but someone might kick it over by mistake. She set it in her knapsack, leaving the top open. It was less visible, at least. But at the end of class, someone in a hurry to get out brushed against it with his foot and it almost tipped over.

This isn't going to be easy, she thought.

Lost Egg

By the time Katie got home from school on the first day of the Eggsperiment, she was already sick of Meg. She set the egg on the kitchen table and poured herself a glass of cider. She hadn't had time to fill in the record sheet since she left Health.

11 A.M.	Earth Science	*Meg in carton*
12 noon	Lunch	*Feeding. Carried Meg in carton*
1 P.M.	French	*Meg on desk in carton*
2 P.M.	Gym	*Meg on top of bleachers*

That had been the worst part of the day. She'd changed into her gymsuit, put her backpack in her locker, and started out toward the gym. Then she'd remembered Meg.

130:

She had to go back and get the carton out of the locker. By the time she walked out on the gym floor, the class was lined up against the wall. She had to walk past everyone carrying the Chinese food container.

"Bring your lunch?" someone wisecracked.

Katie tried to explain to the teacher. "Miss Murphy, I can't leave this in my locker. It's from Health class."

"What?"

"It's an egg, but it's supposed to be a baby. It's a project. It's kind of hard to explain."

The teacher raised her eyebrows. "Hear a new one every day," she said. "As long as you've got on your shorts and sneakers, I'm satisfied. Put the carton somewhere and let's get going."

Katie set it on top of the folded bleachers. It was the farthest she'd been from the egg all day. She found herself looking over every so often to check on it. This is ridiculous, she told herself.

It was three o'clock now, time for another feeding. She listed it on the record sheet and checked the egg. No cracks. She'd agreed to meet Ruth for a bike ride after school.

"Let's go for a long one," Ruth had said. "My grandmother's been on my back, and if I don't let off steam, I'm going to give it right back to her one of these days."

Katie changed into shorts and sneakers. She was on her way out the door to check her tires when she remembered Meg.

"You can't leave the baby alone," Mrs. Ortiz had said.

I don't want to carry this dumb egg along on a bike ride. If I wear a backpack I'll get all sweaty. If I tie it onto the carrier, it might break when I go over bumps.

For a brief moment, she thought of dumping the egg down the disposal.

She finally decided to call Ruth. Maybe her mother would take care of the egg.

"That's the weirdest thing I've ever heard of," Ruth said when Katie described the situation. "My mother's not here, but wait, I'll ask my grandmother."

She returned to the phone in a few seconds. "Granny doesn't understand, but she says it's okay to leave the egg here. She'll make sure no one touches it. She's watching the soaps."

After padding the container with paper towels for extra protection, Katie fit it carefully into her backpack and pedaled to Ruth's.

"This is supposed to be a baby?" Ruth's grandmother asked.

"Yes. Her name is Meg."

"Isn't that cute, an egg named Meg."

Katie wished she had never signed up for Health.

"What am I supposed to do with it?" Ruth's grandmother asked.

"Just don't let anyone touch it. Here. I'll put it up on the bookcase. You won't even have to think about it." She set the carton next to a green vase. "Thanks for taking care of it."

"You're welcome, dear. Now, Ruth, see the way your friend has her hair back out of her eyes? Why can't you do that? It's so much more attractive."

Ruth heaved a sigh but kept her temper. "I know, Granny, I know. We've got to go now."

They left before she could make any more digs.

"What a pain," Ruth said. "All she does is nag and complain. She's driving all of us crazy."

They rode through town, then followed Center Street all the way out. Ruth kept talking about her grandmother.

"She doesn't like our food, and she says we play our music too loud. She likes these stations that play mushy music with a million violins."

It was strange to hear Ruth complain. Her family seemed perfect from the outside. Maybe you never really know what families are like inside, Katie thought.

"Let's stop at the next stand and buy some apples," Ruth called back to her.

They bought cider and oatmeal cookies, too, and sat on the grass near the edge of the road to eat and rest.

Katie gazed out over the fields. Cows grazed next to fat mounds of hay, cut and rolled, waiting to be collected and stored. Overhead, geese, heading south, skimmed across the sky in tight formation.

"We'd better start back," Ruth said. "It's my night to cook."

"What are you making?"

"Hamburgers. Granny will complain, of course. Last week, Mitch made a Mexican dinner with refried beans, tortillas, guacamole, and everything. Granny said it gave her heartburn and kept her up all night. Then Mom and Dad had this argument about whether we should change the way we eat. Mom said, 'Absolutely not!' She bought chicken and turkey frozen dinners and said Granny could eat those when we have hot food. But Dad's still mad." She shook her head. "The whole thing's a mess. We never had fights like this before."

The plaintive, lost note in her voice surprised Katie. In

all the years that they'd been friends, Katie had never seen Ruth so shaky.

"Hey. Don't worry! It will work out," Katie said. "It's just hard when new people join a family. Like Steve in my house. It gets easier. They get used to your ways, and you get used to theirs. Everybody calms down after a while."

Ruth smiled halfheartedly, not really convinced. "Steve's a hundred times better than Granny, Katie."

"I didn't think so last year. He complained about everything."

Ruth stood up and brushed off the seat of her pants. "Let's go."

Katie knew she didn't want to talk about it anymore. Ruth probably wished she hadn't revealed how upset she was.

Katie picked up her egg at Ruth's, and thanked Granny for watching it. She cycled home through the dusk. The lights were on at her house. It always felt nicer to come home when someone was there before her.

Steve was cooking dinner. "Spaghetti and meat sauce. Straight from the jar. Ready in fifteen minutes."

She left her things on the counter and took the stairs two at a time, heading for a shower.

It wasn't until much later that night that she remembered the egg. She thought back carefully. She'd had it in her backpack when she came in. Then she'd taken the carton out and put it on the counter.

She went downstairs and looked in the kitchen. Her backpack was on the floor by the radiator, but there was no sign of the Chinese food container.

She found Steve in the living room watching TV. "Steve,

134:

did you see a white container? I left it in the kitchen before dinner."

He shook his head. "Maddie cleaned up tonight."

Maddie was working at her desk in the upstairs hall. "A Chinese food container? I threw it out."

"In the garbage?"

"Yes, of course, in the garbage. Outside."

Still barefoot, Katie raced out to the garbage can. The grass was ice-cold with dew. She opened the lid and untied the plastic sack inside. Fumes of old coffee grounds and vegetable scraps disgusted her, but she dug around through the damp, mysterious odds and ends until she felt something square and smooth. She pulled up the carton with a sigh of relief. Thank God! She'd found it! Garbage was collected on Wednesday mornings. That would've been the end of Meg Egg.

In the kitchen she washed her hands and wiped the carton with a sponge before checking the egg. Maybe it had cracked. Good thing she'd put in so much foam.

When the carton was reasonably clean, she opened the flaps and looked inside. It was empty! The egg must have fallen out. Maybe it was somewhere in the garbage bag.

Tears came to her eyes. She blinked them back, trying not to panic. Now what could she do? She'd never locate it in the dark. She found a flashlight at the top of the cellar steps and went back out.

Joel will kill me, she thought. We'll flunk the course. She sifted through the entire bag but found not even a broken shell. Now what? she wondered. Panic was beginning to subside, and in its place came a sense of the ridiculous. She had to grin. What a dumb project.

She went back inside, rinsed her hands, and went up-stairs again. "Mom, remember that egg project I told you about? The one where the egg is the baby?"

Maddie nodded absentmindedly, her eyes still on the file she was reading.

"Well, I just lost the baby."

This caught her mother's interest. "What?"

"The baby, the egg. Meg Egg. I lost her. She was on the counter in that Chinese food container, and now she's gone. She's not in the garbage. I don't know where she is." Katie didn't know whether to laugh or cry. It was so silly but serious, too.

Maddie looked puzzled. "You lost the egg? Where was it again?"

"In the carton. Remember I asked you about the carton? You said you threw it out. I found the carton but not the egg."

"Now I remember. I did throw it out, but it was empty."

"Empty? Why didn't you say so?"

"You didn't ask me."

"Well, where could it have gone?"

"Beats me. Oh, sorry, dear. No pun intended. We'd better ask Steve if he's seen it."

They went down to the living room together. Steve was flipping the channels. "Why do they show the same commercial two or three times during the same show? It's an insult to the intelligence."

"Did you see an egg?" Katie asked.

"An egg? I've seen hundreds in my lifetime, but it never developed into anything serious. An egg. You sound like an old girlfriend of mine. 'Want *an* egg for breakfast?' she'd say. Who eats just one egg?"

"This is serious. Did you see a real egg when you were cooking dinner?" Katie asked.

"Katie lost a special egg," Maddie explained.

"Was it round and white, or brown and oval?" Steve couldn't seem to understand the gravity of the situation.

"Steve, stop kidding. This is serious."

"Did I see an egg when I was cooking?" He tried to remember. "Yes, I did. There was an egg on the counter. I couldn't figure out how it got there. So I put it back in the refrigerator."

"The refrigerator!" Katie ran to the kitchen and pulled open the refrigerator door. There it was, sitting next to the other eggs in the rack, illuminated by the bright light. Katie took it out and cupped it in her hands to warm it. "Poor Meg! At least two hours in there. Poor thing," she cooed. "I found her! I don't know what I would've done."

Maddie and Steve had followed her into the kitchen.

"Is she talking about an egg?" Steve asked Maddie.

"It's supposed to be a baby," Maddie explained.

"A baby. Oh. That explains it, of course. The egg is her baby. What does that make you and me, the proud grandparents? You're both losing your minds." He headed back toward the living room. "This conversation makes TV look intelligent."

"Thanks, Mom," Katie said.

"Be more careful next time, okay?"

"Tomorrow's Joel's turn."

Finishing Up

Spending time in the refrigerator wasn't the worst thing that happened to an egg baby on the first day of the project. One team dropped their baby on the cafeteria floor during lunch. The lunch lady made them clean it up with a sponge. One team forgot theirs in a locker overnight. One egg was eaten by a family dog and another was cooked for breakfast.

"Class, this is not a good beginning," said Mrs. Ortiz. "Out of twelve babies, we have three deaths and several near misses. Quite a high infant mortality rate." She gave new eggs to the three teams whose eggs had cracked or been eaten. "Everyone, be more careful!" she cautioned.

Katie gave Meg Egg to Joel with a sigh of relief. "She

needs another feeding at lunch," she said, handing over the record sheets.

That night after dinner, Joel called. "What did you do when you wanted to go out? I had to carry it to soccer practice today. I felt like a jerk."

"It would be worse if it was real," she said. "It might cry all the time and you couldn't leave it on the bench."

"Okay, so it could be worse, but this is bad enough, you know? What about the weekend? I don't want to drag this egg around with me."

"Maybe she'll stop the Eggsperiment on Friday. We can all ask her."

"We could just fake it and fill out the record sheet. Some people are doing that, you know."

Katie didn't know what to say. She wasn't comfortable with that idea.

"I don't want to fake it, either," Joel said finally.

Katie had the egg again on Wednesday. She kept it out of the kitchen and took it with her when she went to her piano lesson. She had this fantasy that the egg would suddenly jump out of its container and begin to dance in time to her piano piece. She giggled. Her piano teacher frowned.

That night at dinner, Katie complained to Maddie. "Are babies really like this? You have to lug them around everywhere? What if you just feel like taking off?"

"You can't," said Maddie. "You can arrange for child care, hire baby-sitters, do things like that. But you have to pay for that, and it isn't always easy. You just get used to having the baby with you, that's all. I remember one time when you were tiny, I went to the city alone to meet a

: 139

friend. I took a train in and started walking toward the restaurant where we were having lunch. I kept thinking that I'd lost something, or left it on the train. I double-checked, and I had my bag. Something was missing, but I couldn't figure out what it was. Finally I realized that it was you. I hadn't been away from you since you were born."

"I never knew it would be like this," Katie said. "Is this the way it's going to be when the baby comes?"

Maddie nodded and smiled. "And this one won't turn back into an egg at the end of a week. It'll be here on the twenty-year-plus plan."

Mrs. Ortiz wouldn't shorten the Eggsperiment. It went right through to Monday. Katie kept Meg Egg on Saturday because Joel had a game. Joel kept her Sunday. On Monday morning, they double-checked the chart and got ready to turn Meg back in.

"We missed three or four feedings," Katie said.

"And there was the night I left it in the basket of my bike. We'll lose points for that," Joel said.

"Not as many as for the refrigerator mix-up at my house," Katie said. "I'm glad it's over. I'm not ready for this much responsibility."

Mrs. Ortiz collected the eggs and charts at the start of class.

"What will you do with them?" asked a girl in the front row.

"I don't know," said Mrs. Ortiz, looking at the egg carton she'd set them in.

"How about an egg fight?" suggested a boy Katie didn't know.

"That's disgusting!" said the girl sitting next to him. "After a week with your egg, you'd just crack it on somebody's head? Where are your feelings?"

"What do you want to do with yours? Send it to nursery school?" he retorted.

"Enough!" said Mrs. Ortiz. "I'll figure something out."

"Don't eat them, Mrs. O.," said another boy.

"I won't, I promise you!" she said.

The last assignment was to write a conclusion explaining what you'd learned from the experiment, in essay or in list form. Katie wrote hers after dinner on Monday night.

1. Babies tie you down. You can't just get up and go whenever you want.

2. People don't realize how much care babies need.

3. It's easy to hurt a baby.

It's even easier to hurt an egg, she thought. Babies don't fit in the refrigerator.

4. It's hard to find other people to take care of your baby.

The last item on the list was a question:

5. Why do people have babies, anyway?

Claire Visits

The postman left the package inside the storm door. It fell out when Katie let herself in after school. She examined the large envelope, soft and squishy, with an unfamiliar return address in the city. *Miss Katie Henderson,* it said. Upstairs, sitting on her bed, she pulled it open and slid out a tissue-wrapped bundle with a letter from Claire.

"Dear Katie, I found this at a flea market downtown. Rummaging around reminded me of our shopping trip. Doesn't this have great lace? The color is just jazzy enough. You can wear it under regular clothes and no one but you will know that you're secretly a vamp."

Katie unfolded the slip and held it up, deep rose with a border of creamy lace flowers. Claire can really find things, she thought.

The letter continued: "Last week, I saw another dance troupe, called City Lights. In one dance, the lights were off and only a candle burned in the center of the stage. The dancers wore silver suits that reflected the flame. It was eerie.

"Ed's developed the pictures he took while you were here. You look terrific!

"I have to come out your way for a business seminar that ends around four. I'd love to see you. Could we have dinner? I can pick you up at your house and get you back early enough for a school night. Call me and let me know."

The date she named was the next Wednesday. When Katie told Maddie the plan, Maddie raised her eyebrows.

"This will be interesting," she said.

"What will?" Katie felt protective. Claire was her friend.

"I've never met any of Ed's women friends," Maddie said.

"Claire's the only one I've met," Katie said. "She's great, you'll see."

But Maddie wasn't home from work yet when Claire rang the bell. She looked just the same as Katie remembered, curly hair almost out of control, and just a hint of makeup. Her clothes were fancier, though.

"My business disguise," Claire joked.

They ate at a small restaurant overlooking a duck pond. Since it was early, the restaurant was almost empty. They chose a window table.

Claire ordered a glass of wine for herself and Perrier for Katie. They watched the ducks slowly circle the pond, rippling the dark surface.

Katie described high school and told Claire about the

Eggsperiment, making her laugh so hard that she had to wipe her eyes.

"Tell that story to Ed! He'll crack up. Oh, what an awful pun. I'm sorry."

"I'll tell him at Thanksgiving."

"Good, then I can hear it again. I'll be there, too. And your grandmother's coming."

"It will be like a real holiday, then. Have you met Grandma?"

"Ed took me out to see her last weekend." Claire shook her head. "You wouldn't believe how nervous I was. You know, going to meet the mother and all that. You can never tell what it will be like."

Katie nodded. Claire always made her feel so grown up. Here she was, talking to her as if she would understand the whole situation.

"But it went smoothly. I like your grandmother very much. She's so spunky! But elegant, too. I think she liked me." Claire grinned like a little kid describing a new friend made at school.

When they got back to the house, Claire went in with Katie. She shook hands easily with Maddie and Steve, and admired the house. Maddie even showed her the baby's room.

"Some people say it's bad luck to get prepared early," Maddie said.

Claire nodded. "I've heard that, too, but I don't believe it. Anyway, I can't stand last-minute rushing."

Maddie smiled. "That's exactly how I feel!"

After Claire had left, Maddie said, "What a nice woman."

144:

Katie agreed. "Isn't she easy to talk to?"

"She seems very fond of you."

"We had fun together in the city."

"I hope Ed's smart enough to hold on to her," Maddie said. "She'd be good for him."

Katie didn't really understand what Maddie meant, but she hoped Claire would stay around, too. Not for Ed's sake, but for her own.

The Fall

September passed quickly. Katie had field hockey practice three afternoons a week, and piano lessons on Wednesdays. Homework took a lot more time than it had in eighth grade. And every week she wrote to Paul. In turn, he wrote her long, funny letters about classmates, courses, things on his mind. His letters came on Tuesdays, usually, written on yellow paper from a legal pad, with a sloppy script that reminded Katie of the way he walked. She wrote back on Tuesday night or Wednesday, often enclosing a cartoon or a funny headline from the news or a magazine ad. "You can't do better than this," one ad said. After she'd sent it, she felt embarrassed but hoped he'd know she meant it as a joke.

Maddie kept on going to work, even though she was uncomfortable. She wore support stockings to help her legs and lay down for a while every day when she got home from work.

"Maybe you should quit early and take it easy," Steve suggested. "It's not a question of equal rights or anything like that. You don't see me going in every day carrying thirty extra pounds. You don't have to prove to anyone that you're Superwoman, you know."

But Maddie wouldn't even consider it. "I'm fine," she insisted. "I told you, I'm like those pioneer women who plowed all day and then went home and gave birth. I'll be at work until those labor pains hit."

At the end of September, Steve had a business trip that couldn't be postponed. "Are you sure you're okay?" he asked Maddie again and again.

"I'm fine! We've got at least four more weeks. Besides, Katie's here with me, so there's nothing to worry about."

Katie wasn't sure how she could help, but Maddie's words made her proud.

Monday and Tuesday night felt a lot like the old days when it was just Maddie and Katie living together. Monday they made club sandwiches and played double solitaire for money. Tuesday they went to see two Fred Astaire–Ginger Rogers movies. Afterward, Maddie tried a few dance steps out on the sidewalk, but her weight threw her off balance. If she hadn't caught hold of a lamppost, she might have fallen.

"I wonder if Ginger Rogers was ever pregnant," she said. "I bet not."

"Be careful, Mom," Katie said. "Take it easy, okay?"

On Wednesday afternoon the phone rang.

"Katie, it's me, honey." Maddie's voice was high and shaky. "I'm at the hospital. I had a fall. The baby's okay. Dr. Sunderland is here with me. We've checked the heartbeat. I started to have contractions, and they're trying to stop them."

Katie listened but found it hard to take it all in. It seemed like time stopped in one instant. She had to remind herself to breathe in and out.

"I tried to reach Steve, but he's not at the hotel. I'll keep trying. Katie, sweetheart, would you come over and be with me?"

The note of pleading in Maddie's voice brought Katie back to life.

"Sure, Mom. I'll take a cab. I'll bring some stuff—your robe and nightgown. Anything else?"

Maddie thought of a few more things. It took Katie only a few minutes to pack the yellow duffel bag that Maddie always used for her leotard and gym things. She was waiting on the sidewalk when the cab turned the corner.

Usually, cabs made her feel fancy and grown up. She'd pretend to be a celebrity or a rich lady with a chauffeur. But today she was too worried to fantasize.

How had Maddie fallen? Had someone pushed into her? Maybe she'd tripped and lost her balance again.

When the cab reached the hospital, Katie paid the driver and hurried in, past the urns of chrysanthemums, right toward the elevator.

"Miss! Miss! Just a minute, miss. You need a guest pass." The lady at the information desk wore a pale-blue smock, pink glasses with gold speckles, and a heart-shaped pin that said "Volunteer." "Children under fourteen must be accompanied by an adult," she said, adjusting her glasses and inspecting Katie as if she were a specimen.

"I am fourteen," Katie said. "I'm here to see my mother."

"Oh. I see." From the sound of the woman's voice, Katie could tell that she didn't believe her.

"I'm in high school. I turned fourteen last spring. I'd like a pass, please." Katie struggled to keep her voice calm.

"What floor is your mother on, dear?"

"I don't know. Her name is Madeline Norton."

The woman checked her file, moving so slowly that Katie thought she'd scream if she had to wait a minute more.

"Room 6E," Pink Glasses finally said, and handed Katie a pass.

Maddie lay with her eyes closed, her face pale against the white pillow. With her hair brushed back off her forehead, she looked almost like a child. Only the mound of her stomach and the few strands of gray in her dark hair marked her age.

Katie tiptoed in, trying not to wake her, but Maddie's eyes flickered open and she smiled.

"Hi, sweetheart." She held out her hand.

Katie pulled the metal armchair up to the side of the bed and sat close enough to hold her mother's hand.

"How do you feel?"

"Sleepy. Tired. A little less panicked, now that Dr. Sutherland thinks everything's going to be fine."

"What happened?"

"You know what a klutz I can be. I tripped on the carpet at work. I had my arms full of files and I went right over!

Landed on top of the files and my poor belly here." She patted the mound under the sheet. "When I felt the contractions start, I got scared."

Maddie ran her hand gently over the covers on top of her belly as if to calm and soothe it.

"They stopped the contractions by giving me this IV. But they might start again. The baby's at least four weeks early. There might be complications if it's born so soon. The longer I can hold off the birth, the stronger it will be."

Maddie rambled on, fueled by panic. Katie listened but her mind wandered. She didn't understand all the details about the baby, but it scared her to see her mother so vulnerable. She was so used to Maddie's being strong and stubborn, not confused and shaken like this.

After a while Maddie dozed off, still holding on to Katie's hand. In the silence of the room, Katie could hear tinny, irritating waves of canned laughter from the television across the hall. Rubber-soled shoes squeaked briskly past the door. Occasional buzzes and beeps came from intercoms, and in the distance elevator doors rumbled open and then closed.

Maddie seemed to be sleeping soundly, so Katie gently disengaged her hand and tiptoed out into the hall. It was 5:35 on the clock at the nurses' station. She decided to call Mrs. Ives. Maddie had arranged for her to sleep over at Ruth's.

She dialed Ruth's number and Mrs. Ives answered after just one ring.

"Oh Katie, I'm so glad it's you. I tried to reach you at the house, but I guess you'd already left. How's your mother?"

150:

"She's sleeping now. She's pretty shaken up."

It felt so odd to be discussing Maddie this way, as if she were an equal instead of her mother.

"We're just about to sit down to dinner. Would you like me to come and get you now, or would you rather stay a little longer?"

Imagining the cheerful normalcy of the Iveses' dinner table, Katie was tempted to go. But she couldn't leave Maddie alone for the whole evening. It wasn't even six yet.

"I'd better stay. Visiting hours are over at eight o'clock."

When Katie got back, Maddie was sitting up eating soup. She had more color in her face now.

"I called Mrs. Ives," Katie said. "She's coming over later."

Maddie lay back against the pillow. A wave of pain crossed her face. She placed her hands on her stomach. "Hope that's just a cramp," she said.

Katie sat down on the edge of the armchair and watched her mother nervously. She didn't know how to help.

"Should I get the nurse?" she said.

Maddie shook her head, but tears oozed out of the corners of her eyes. She began to sob silently.

Uncertainly, Katie took her hand.

Maddie spoke softly. "I just don't want to lose this baby. I might not get another chance. Steve wants kids so badly. And here I am messing it all up."

The sobs choked her. She coughed for a minute, then Katie asked, "Can you reach the Kleenex?"

Katie put the box beside her arm. Maddie fumbled for one and finally pulled out a handful. She wiped her eyes.

"I don't know what got into me," she apologized.

"It's natural to be upset. Who wouldn't be?"

"Thanks, sweetheart." Maddie patted Katie's hand. She had control of herself again. "I guess it was just a cramp. I could use something to read. Think you could go down and pick me up some magazines? Good and junky, okay?"

Katie knew just what she wanted. She went down to the gift shop, and when she got back, a nurse was taking Maddie's blood pressure.

"This is my daughter, Katie," Maddie introduced her.

The nurse nodded. "Going to be a big sister soon, huh?"

Katie nodded back. What a jerk! Soon? How soon? That was the problem, wasn't it?

Fortunately the nurse finished up quickly and left before saying anything else dumb.

"What time is it?" Maddie asked.

"Ten after seven."

"I want to try Steve again. Can you hand me the phone?"

Katie placed it next to her on the bed. Maddie dialed and waited, then set the receiver down. "He must be out at dinner. I hoped I could reach him while you were here." She smiled almost shyly. "I'm a little worried about how to tell him. You can give me moral support."

Katie looked out the dark window. She didn't want to be there when Maddie told Steve. The baby was theirs. She didn't want to butt in or even have to listen to the conversation.

Maddie was watching her, reading her face.

"I thought it would be nice for all of us to be together and share the news. The baby's a part of all of us. We're family. It's at times like these that family counts more than ever, right? We're there for each other."

Katie looked down at her sneakers for a minute, letting the words sink in. Maddie wanted her there because they were a family, all three of them. No, all four of them. Or almost four.

She picked up the receiver and handed it to Maddie. "Let's try one more time. Maybe he's back from dinner."

Steve Gets Home

Steve flew home the next morning. He left a note for Katie at the house: "I'm at the hospital. Call me and I'll pick you up."

Katie called as soon as she came home from school. In less than half an hour, Steve beeped the car horn outside. They stopped to get daisies and dried apricots, Maddie's favorites.

Maddie was asleep when they arrived.

"Let's go down to the coffee shop and I'll tell you what the doctor said," Steve suggested.

When the waitress brought their order, Steve began to describe what the doctor had told him. But he didn't really understand it well himself.

"It has something to do with the fall triggering contractions. These tests are to see if the baby's all right. They use this sonar test to get a picture of where it is, what position it's in, and to see if the placenta's still connected. Apparently, it looks okay. But then they're testing the fluid to check the levels of the enzyme or the salt or something. See? I can't get it straight. I think they're trying to predict if the contractions are going to start again."

Katie listened and watched his face as he talked. She'd never thought much about his feelings before. As she looked at him groping for words, fumbling to explain what the doctor had said, he wasn't just any nice-looking, dark-haired man, not just some man her mother liked. He was Steve. Her stepfather. The father of the baby that would be her brother or her sister.

All the wrinkles on his face were deep today, the smile lines around his mouth, the tiny Vs in the corners of his eyes, the creases between his eyebrows, the short, straight lines across his forehead. He didn't look boyish. He looked frightened. Suddenly she understood. Steve loved Maddie. He was frightened because he really loved her. And he couldn't do anything to help her. He just had to sit here and wait.

He hates waiting, she thought. He likes to get things done, to solve things and get on to something else.

"After the tests, all we can do is wait it out. No more work for Maddie, though. That's out. No housework, either. We have to make her take that seriously, okay? We can gang up on her, keep her out of the kitchen and off her feet. It won't be easy."

Katie nodded and grinned. "If she weren't so pregnant, we could threaten to sit on her."

But they didn't have to gang up on Maddie, after all. She

was scared, and she followed the doctor's orders docilely. She came home the next morning and let Steve get her settled upstairs in their bedroom. He moved in a card table and set it up next to the bed. When she felt up to it, she worked for an hour or so. But she napped a lot. In the evening she listened to the news while Steve and Katie made dinner.

It was just as well that Maddie wasn't downstairs to watch the two of them.

"Abbott and Costello in the kitchen," Steve said. "Oh, Ollie, what a mess you've gotten me into," he whined, scratching the top of his head and making a long face. "No, that's Laurel and Hardy. Same idea, right?"

Steve had on one of Maddie's aprons, tied high up under his arms. He was frying meatballs, oblivious to the grease splattering all over the top of the stove. Katie was working on the sauce. She had sautéed onions and garlic and now was stirring in chopped tomatoes. She sprinkled basil over the whole surface.

"Easy, girl, easy," Steve cautioned, fanning the spice away from his face.

"Mom says you can never have enough garlic or basil," Katie told him.

"That's her opinion. Temperance, my dear, temperance."

Katie went right on with her own scheme. She sliced up a large zucchini and a green pepper and slid them into the pan. Steve watched with one eyebrow raised.

"Is that a recipe you're following?" he asked.

"Yes. It's in *Vegetarian Delectables.*"

"You're making tomato sauce from that piece of California propaganda? You expect my meatballs to feel at home with those lumpy vegetables in the sauce?"

"It'll be good. Don't worry. Just make the pasta."

Not wholly satisfied, Steve drained his meatballs and went back to the table, where he'd assembled the flour and eggs needed for pasta. "Now you're not going to believe this, Miss Know-It-All Home Economics Whiz, but I make this dough without even using a bowl."

Katie didn't answer, but she did look up to watch. Steve shaped the flour into a cone shape. "Like a little volcano, see?" Then he broke eggs into the depression at the top and, using a fork, began to mix in the eggs gradually, trying to keep the sides of the volcano firm, so the egg mixture wouldn't spill out onto the table. "Careful, now. Oh, no. Careful, boy. Uh-oh, it's cresting the edge. Move quick, that's it, keep it moving. Keep that fork going." He kept up a monologue of coaching tips as he struggled to contain the batter. Slowly the mixture grew in size, consuming the flour until it turned into a lump of sticky dough. "Perfection!" he exclaimed, kissing his fingertips, and leaving a floury mustache above his mouth.

He shaped the dough into a yellow ball, rolled it out in a thin sheet, and draped it over the back of a chair to dry.

"We could have used spaghetti," Katie said, looking at the flour on the floor, the sticky countertop, the dusting of flour all over Steve's clothes.

"That dry stuff in the cardboard box? Those thin little sticks? Those tasteless toothpicks? The great chef can take such abuse no longer. Out, out, you peasant, get out." He pushed her toward the kitchen door with little shoves. "Go to the store and get me some good wine vinegar. I can't make a decent salad dressing without it."

Two blocks away was a tiny convenience store with narrow, jammed aisles and wooden floors. Ever since she was old enough to cross streets by herself, Katie had come here for bubble gum or Tootsie Roll pops, or ice cream in the summer.

She bought the vinegar and walked back along the familiar blocks, looking in the windows of the houses. In some, the curtains were drawn, but in others, she could see people sitting on couches reading the paper or watching the news on TV. The families looked so secure, as if nothing bad could ever threaten their well-lit evening serenity.

But there's no guarantee, Katie thought. You could fall, as Maddie had. You could get hit by a truck or break a leg. Anything could happen. She'd learned a lot these past months. It wasn't just Maddie's fall. It was Grandma's being so sick, too. When you're little, they don't let you know about the bad things that go on. Maybe that was good, maybe not. She wasn't sure.

She thought about the baby. Girl or boy? A girl, she hoped.

She passed her favorite house—the Castle, she'd always called it. It was made of fieldstone, with a porch, turrets, and diamond-paned windows. The old couple who used to live there had given out cider and powdered doughnuts on Halloween. But they'd moved away, retired to Florida or California. Now there was a new family with little kids. Maybe her sister would be friends with them. She'd rollerskate on the street and climb the same backyard trees that Katie had.

And she'll believe that the world is safe and nothing can

bother you as long as the light is on, Katie thought. I hope she believes in Santa until she's seven—or six, at least.

Up ahead she could see the lights of her own house. Steve was waiting, she rememberd. Hitching the bag up higher, she speeded up, serious thoughts pushed aside by visions of fresh pasta and meatballs.

Waiting

"Two weeks down, two to go," Maddie groaned, and she rolled onto her side, trying to get comfortable.

"I can get you some tea," Katie offered.

"No, that's okay."

Maddie closed her eyes. She seemed to be falling asleep again. Katie waited a few minutes, then tiptoed out, closing the door silently behind her.

She went into her room to answer a letter from Paul that had come in the mail that morning. She reread it, sitting at her desk. The letter was cheerful but kind of bland until the last two pages. Then, all of a sudden, it got romantic. Mushy. Sort of wistful.

"There's a song on the radio now. I think it's from the

sixties. It's saying a lot of nice things about this guy's girl, like she's honey, sunshine, stuff like that. I'm sitting here listening to it and I'm thinking of you, wishing I could hold you close right now and say these things to you. You're my girl, right? I hope you are. I think about you every day and every night. And I think about the time we spent together. Mostly I think about kissing you. And I hope you think about me."

Katie read it again. If he'd sent it six weeks ago, she would have felt terrific. Right after she came home from Grandma's, he'd been in her mind all the time. Back then she could honestly say she felt the same way. But now, reading the letter made her feel slightly uncomfortable, even nervous. The summer felt far away. And ever since the Eggsperiment, she'd stayed friendly with Joel. She wouldn't be surprised if he asked her out. She'd like to go out with him. If she could just get her courage up, she'd ask him out herself.

So what could she say to Paul? She took out her stationery box and rummaged through it. Maybe the right card would make it easier. She found one with two little kids standing next to each other; they had grimy knees and scuffed sneakers, shorts that were wrinkled, T-shirts smudged with jelly, paint, and dirt. One had a plastic pail over his head—bright red plastic, the kind you use at the beach. For some reason, the card reminded her of the two of them. Anyway, it was funny.

She stared at the card awhile, trying to think of something to say. She couldn't be all romantic in return. It wouldn't be honest.

She heard Steve's car pull into the driveway below. The

car door slammed shut, and she heard his footsteps on the gravel. Maybe she'd get more ideas if she waited until after dinner.

By the time she got downstairs, Steve had hung up his coat and was pulling his tie loose.

"Hi, Katie," he said. He didn't kiss her or even hug her in greeting. Even though Maddie's fall had made them closer, some formality remained.

"Mom's asleep," Katie said.

"I'll tiptoe in and get changed. What'll we have for dinner?"

Cooking together was something they both had come to enjoy. The blind leading the blind, Steve called it. No-fail cooking. "How can we fail? Neither one of us knows anything, and there's nobody else to judge." They tried anything. Italian, Chinese, French, even vegetarian.

"I got a taco kit," Katie said.

"Add water, and presto! *ta da!* Tacos emerge from the box!"

Katie just shook her head. He loved to kid. Funny, she'd never noticed last year.

"You start and I'll be done in a few minutes."

Katie got out the vegetables and began to chop onions.

"Okay, what can I do to help?" Steve asked.

"Put the taco shells in the oven to warm."

"Easy! I like this kind of meal. So what's new? How's school? Get any more of that hot mail from prep school?"

Steve often kidded her about Paul's letters, but today she didn't feel like laughing.

"I did get a letter today," she said. "But it was kind of weird."

162:

Maybe Steve would know what she should do. A few weeks ago she wouldn't have dared ask him.

"How so, weird?"

She hesitated, searching for the right word. "It was romantic. Mushy. Too mushy."

"Passionate? The boy's got taste—what can I say?"

"Steve! It wasn't passionate, it was just too romantic, that's all."

"How can something be *too* romantic?"

"Because I don't feel like that. It makes me nervous."

"Ah! I see. He likes you but you don't like him anymore."

"Not like that. I still like him, but I don't sit around thinking about him all the time. It's been almost two months since I've seen him."

Steve nodded. "Simple. It's a case of boarding-school love. Paul's at school, a little bored, a little lonely. He's got these nice summer memories. So he plays them over again in his mind. If he weren't away at that school, he probably would've met other people, too. He's daydreaming, that's all. Don't be scared by it. Just accept the compliment. Feelings are like shadows, Katie. They come and go. You can't predict how you're going to feel from minute to minute. You may see him over Thanksgiving and come back with your eyes shining."

"But what should I do about writing back?"

"Just write back the way you always do."

Steve was setting the kitchen table for two. "When I first met your mother, we had a few meetings about a project. I liked her right away. Sometimes that happens, just like the songs say. But I kept it to myself for a while. I didn't want to scare her off. First we had lunch, but we didn't talk about the project. We were eating Italian food. I remember we traded techniques for getting the spaghetti onto the fork and into your mouth. The twirl-it-on-the-fork method. The scoop-and-slurp method. The cut-it-with-your-fork, chicken-out way.

"Now, how many people can you discuss these things with? I would have proposed right there in the Villa Romana. But take it slow, I told myself. After a while, I could tell that she liked me. So I let on how I was feeling. Slow. Like a light rain."

Steve's fingers danced through the air as if they were raindrops, and he did a little soft-shoe.

Katie groaned. "You sound like one of those movies from the 1940s."

"I'm not that old, infant. Too bad, I was just getting into it."

"That's what I was afraid of."

After dinner, Katie wrote to Paul, and it wasn't as hard as she'd expected. She told him that she'd be in the city, at her father's apartment, for Thanksgiving. Maybe they could get together then, she suggested.

Before she went to bed, she went in to say goodnight to her mother. Maddie was propped up on pillows, reading. Katie sat down on the edge of the bed.

"I think Steve's going to be a good father," she told Maddie.

"Maybe you're giving him good practice," Maddie suggested, reaching over to smooth Katie's hair. "You're the coach."

"I don't think you guys need any coaching."

Maddie squeezed Katie's hand. "If this baby turns out to be as nice as you, I'll be very proud."

Katie nestled her head against her mother's shoulder and sat like that for a few minutes, enjoying the warmth and the praise. She wasn't afraid of the baby anymore. And she wasn't angry, either. The anger had just evaporated. It was hard to remember why she'd ever been so mad. Steve was right about feelings. They did come and go.

Plenty to Be Thankful For

The baby was born on a Tuesday. Steve called Katie almost as soon as she walked in the door from school.

"It's a girl! Cute as they come. I guess every father says that, right?"

Actually, the baby was reddish and wrinkly, with her features flattened.

"That's from the birth. She'll smooth out," Maddie said. "You did."

She was right. Within a week, the baby's skin was creamy pink-and-white, like one of the big lilies that bloomed at Grandma's in July. The baby and Maddie both slept on and off during the day, waking up for feedings and walks.

166:

"I'll never get back in shape at this rate," Maddie groaned. "But these nighttime feedings are killing me."

Even though she complained, an air of contentment permeated the whole house. Katie could feel it everywhere, not just in the baby's room, but everywhere. It came from the sounds the baby made as she sucked, soft noises of pleasure and satisfaction. It came even from the sight of Maddie's full breasts, exposed for the feedings. Katie had thought she'd find that embarrassing, but it was the most natural thing she could imagine. It came from the look of delight that lit Steve's face as he watched his new daughter, and from the careful way he held her. All the things Katie had dreaded—the mess of powder and ointment, the sour smell of diapers, the clutter, the noise from crying and cooing—surprised her with pleasure. She loved holding her sister, loved the sense of purpose that the baby gave everyone.

Elizabeth was her name. "Lots of possibilities for nicknames, depending on her personality," Maddie said. "Lizzie, Lisa, Beth, Betsy, Liz, Eliza."

"Beebee, Button, Lizard, Lulu," Steve suggested.

"Elizabeth is nice just the way it is," Katie said. She was thinking of introducing herself as Katherine. It seemed more mature.

The baby was almost four weeks old by Thanksgiving. Katie brought pictures with her when she went to Ed's. This time the train ride into the city went fast.

Ed met her by the clock again. The station was jammed with travelers heading out of the city for the holiday or returning from school.

She spotted her father when he was only halfway across

the station, dodging back and forth through the crowd without breaking stride, his army jacket replaced by a floppy tweed overcoat that ended halfway between his knees and his ankles.

He hugged her and she could smell a spicy combination of pipe tobacco and mothballs in the rough fiber of his coat.

"SO glad you're here," Ed said. "What a great Thanksgiving this will be. Grandma's coming tomorrow."

When they opened the door to the apartment, Katie smelled a cake baking. Claire was rinsing out the bowl. She dried her hands and gave Katie a kiss.

"You look terrific! You look much older, somehow. Really!"

Katie took her bag into the side room. Ed had set up the cot again and cleared away his things to make room for her. She unpacked her clothes and folded the duffel bag, sliding it under the cot. She glanced at the bulletin board and stopped in surprise. Pictures of her covered every inch, shots that Ed had taken last summer, on the ferry, in the park, looking at sculpture outside the museum.

She stared, trying to decide if she liked the way she looked. It was different from looking in a mirror. With a mirror she could change her expression, tilt her head in a different way, work around the image instead of just looking directly at it. In photos, she had to look at herself more objectively; she couldn't change the way she looked.

She looked happy in most, relaxed or enthralled by new sights. In a few, a frown sharpened her face. But in one, the sadness jumped out at her. She looked lost, or abandoned, as if no one anywhere cared about her. It shocked her. She couldn't remember feeling that sad.

The next day, Claire came over after breakfast, and preparations for dinner started. Katie set the table. Claire piled fruit in the center and surrounded it with a circle of candles. When Grandma arrived at a little after two, the apartment smelled delicious.

Grandma handed Ed the pie she was carrying, put the bouquet of dried grasses and flowers on the counter, and hugged Katie. "How does it feel to be a big sister? I want to hear all about the baby, and high school, too."

They all sat down in the living room. Claire put Grandma's bouquet in a clay vase on the mantel. Katie showed the pictures of Elizabeth.

Ed looked them over. "She looks like you, Katie. This is the way you used to smile, a big gummy grin just like this."

Soon it was time to eat. Grandma made the gravy. Ed carved the turkey. Katie dressed the salad. Claire put the vegetables on the table, with the cranberry sauce and the rolls and butter. Then they all sat down.

Ed said grace. "We give thanks for family and for friends, for the changes and the growing that each year brings. We ask for peace, adventure, and contentment in the year to come. Amen."

"Edward, where did you ever hear a grace like that?" Grandma said. "Adventure? I've never heard of such a thing."

"Mom, you love it! If I asked you what you wanted most right now, it would probably be a boat ride down the Nile. You can't fool me."

"The Nile would be lovely. Is this a hint? My Christmas vacation, a present from you?"

"Not this Christmas. We need you right here. We need

both of you. Should we tell them now?" he asked Claire, who nodded.

Katie knew what he was going to say before he began. Ever since she'd arrived, she'd noticed a different feeling between them. Something was settled; some question had been answered.

"Claire and I are getting married at Christmas."

Claire reached over and took Katie's hand. "What do you think?"

"It's great. You like each other a lot."

Ed nodded. "That's the truth. I guess that's why we decided to do it."

Grandma lifted her glass. "A toast. Claire, I've got to tell you, dear, I had given up on Ed's ever settling down. I am delighted!"

Claire smiled. "I'm not sure he'll ever settle down, but we'll manage."

"Wait a minute," Ed objected. "You sound as if I were the original rolling stone."

"Maybe not the original, but a healthy example," said his mother.

Katie listened to the banter with a smile. What a difference from the time when Maddie had told her her wedding plans. Then she'd felt scared and left out. This time she was genuinely happy.

After dinner, they took a cab downtown to see the loft that Ed and Claire had bought.

"We can't fit in Ed's, and my apartment's just as small," Claire said.

It was on the top floor of a warehouse near the river. The sun was setting when the elevator opened onto the huge room. From the tall windows, Katie could see the lights of the city.

As they walked around the empty space, Ed described their plans.

"This corner will be my studio. I'll put the darkroom over here against these pipes. The rest of the space will be for living. We'll put in a few walls, for closets and bookshelves. The kitchen will be in the middle, with the bathroom on the other side. Living room and dining room over in that corner, with the view of the river. At night you can see the boats going up the river, and the lights from the bridge are spectacular."

"We figure there's room for three bedrooms along the other wall. Katie, one of these rooms is set aside for you. Maybe next summer you'll be able to stay longer. And maybe later you'll decide on a city college."

"Now wait a minute," Grandma said. "Don't you go stealing my summertime."

Back home, they had pie and coffee. Grandma left at a little after nine and Ed, Claire, and Katie played Scrabble for a while on the rug in front of the fire.

"No fireplace in the loft," Claire said.

"We'll put in a wood stove, the kind that opens up in front to let you watch the flames," Ed answered. "Whatever your heart desires," he teased.

"How about a U right now?"

"Stuck with a Q, huh? Tough luck, lady."

Claire finally picked a U by herself, and made "qualm." But Katie still won the game. She'd concentrated on fitting letters into the tiny places, making new words by adding one or two letters. New additions changed the originals

and filled the board with words all linked and intercon-
nected.

After the game, Ed walked Claire home, and Katie
watched the fire die down. Tomorrow she'd meet Paul by
the clock in the station. Maybe they'd go to the museum.
Or the zoo. She'd wear the clothes she'd found in the secondhand store with Claire. Ruth had lent her a tie that
looked great with the black jacket.

She thought about Claire and about the wedding. She
knew she'd be more comfortable than she'd been at Maddie's wedding. It didn't have anything to do with what she
would wear, either. It had to do with room.

She used to think there wasn't enough room for her. Not
with Maddie and Steve. Not at Ed's. She just hadn't fit
anywhere. Why not? she wondered.

Now she could see herself in many places. At home with
Maddie, Steve, and Elizabeth. With Ed and Claire in the
new loft. At Grandma's. Yes, always at Grandma's, no
matter what happened.

Before I hated all the changes. I wanted a family like the
ones in books, a mom and a dad, some kids, all living forever in a little white house with shutters. That's the way
it's supposed to be.

Says who? she wondered. Families aren't like that. People change. Everybody does. But that doesn't mean we
stop caring about each other.

She thought of Elizabeth. It had only been a day since
she'd seen her, but she missed her.

She'll be three when I finish high school, Katie thought.
She'll know who I am. Maybe then I'll be ready for a
change myself. College in the city might be fun.

172:

The fire had died down, so that only a few big embers glowed in the ash. She stirred them with the poker and put the screen in front of the fireplace. Then, leaving one light on for Ed, she went to bed, feeling happy and very much at home.

Christine McDonnell graduated from Barnard College and the Columbia University School of Library Service. She has worked as a teacher and children's librarian, as well as a writer of children's books. She currently teaches high school in Brookline, Massachusetts. She lives with her family in Boston.